SPRING CITY FREE LIBRARY
4636
The sound of the weir
FI

D1117088

THE SOUND of the WEIR

THE SOUND of the WEIR

By Mary Ingate

A NOVEL OF SUSPENSE

DODD, MEAD & COMPANY · NEW YORK

ISBN: 0–396–06921–5
Library of Congress Catalog Card Number: 73–19080
Printed in the United States of America
by The Haddon Craftsmen, Inc., Scranton, Penna.

". . . nor all thy Piety nor Wit
  Shall lure it back to cancel half a Line,
Nor all thy Tears wash out a Word of it."

The Rubáiyát of Omar Khayyám of Naishápúr

THE SOUND
of the
WEIR

Chapter 1

My husband is with the Egyptian girl again. He smiles and waves, and she glances upwards at the balcony, her golden body stuck with sand, her striped yellow red and black bikini slashed across lean hips. How old is she? The body ripens early in the hot Greek sun. They run, picking their way among the reclining bodies of the sophisticated morning crowd, to the glinting, sparkling sea. My second husband—a man of forty-five with the hard brown body and laughing eyes of a boy of twenty—a poor bargain he has made, for all my money. But he does not now have to work in the gruelling sun, or tramp with tourists around the archaeological digs. I can see myself in the long mirror on the wall across the room, my wheelchair a dark shape backed by the delicate tracery of the balcony, the bright sky. Immobility does funny things. Since my accident and paralysis from the waist down, my face looks placid, kind, gentle, with a childlike smile. Even now, at sixty, my face is unlined, the eyes wide, incongruous over the shapeless bulk of my body.

The transition from radiant health and running feet, to this, is so sudden. The difference between my husband's thirty years and my forty-five did not seem much at that moment before, on that fateful day, when I stood on the edge of the deep dig, the cliff, and felt a switch of breeze, a caress, at my back before I fell and saw my husband's anxious, horrified face above me.

"Get by the sea," my husband and stepdaughter, Petra, had said when they persuaded me to buy this villa and sell the big dark house among the trees by the archaeological digs. "The sun and light will do you good."

Now I watch from this balcony day after day, my hands idle in my lap.

Petra rises, near naked, from the centre of the ring of reclining young men. She stands erect against the background of the sea and the sky. She turns and gives a wave to the balcony, dark hair flying, then rushes to the sparkling water, Petra, at sixteen, with a fresh young man day after day, perhaps night after night. I shut my eyes to it. For I know what a hand, whosever hand, can do to a virgin body, how it can enslave, forgetful of the mind, the intellect, the spirit. No, let her get over it and break through into the sunshine, forgetting whose hand.

"Mother is writing a novel," Petra called, when I asked her to buy exercise books, pencils and rubber.

"Good, it will do her good."

No, it is not a novel. The laughter, the hot sunshine drifts in, the voices of youth, the yellowness, the sparkle. But yesterday I had an intense memory. This water laps gently, but I heard the sound of the weir, a rushing tide.

Chapter 2

I was thirteen when Miranda married. She was the motherless child of my father's brother, the lackadaisical black sheep who had married an Irish girl during the troubles. She flitted in and out of my childhood but my only clear memory was of a tall girl with thick black hair running on long legs across the fields, her arms outstretched into the wind.

Suddenly we heard that she had, astonishingly, married a widower. My mother went to see for herself. She came back, at first speechless. I can see her vaguely, in the kitchen, taking the pins from her hat.

"Well, a good solid home, with good solid money."

She paused for a moment, watching my father, silent, bent at the table, laboriously reading the farming paper, then turned to the sink.

"And a gentleman, a real gentleman."

I had been asked to visit them in the summer holiday.

Miranda was waiting outside when the old taxi brought me to the stone steps leading to the white canopied door. She fell on me like an excited puppy. Together we raced up the stairs. We ran through the rooms and then out into the gardens.

"Look, isn't it beautiful! What do you think of this?" The gatehouse, the terraces, the boathouse—the place was for me a heaven of delight. The tall mill house, converted to a private country place, smelt faintly of flour. The river, gliding between the garden and the marshes, was crossed by a rustic bridge, high in the middle, like the route of escape on a willow-patterned plate. It crashed further along over the fall and we rushed along the bank to watch the fish, swift pointed arrows, on the ridge and in the wide curtain of water as it fell foaming onto grey granite rocks, then calmed and slid smoothly, green-ridged glass, over a slight dip into the deep mill pool, black, weedy, bottomless.

We met Mr. Montague, I never called him anything else, coming from the rose garden. He was tall and silver-haired and shook my hand with faintly smiling courtesy. His fingers were dry, the bones thinly covered. When speaking, his lips did not move or part and when he was silent, they folded into a single line which I found most endearing. He wore tweed knickerbockers and a Norfolk jacket and had very thin legs encased in thick woolly stockings. I learned later that, when going to look at the young cattle which he kept on the marshes, a tweed deerstalker was pulled over his ears.

I admired him immensely.

Miranda and I tumbled and splashed in the water, and I looked to see if he was watching, then thrashed my arms and showed off my breast stroke. He did not swim. But every morning he rowed me up the river while Miranda, her dark hair bouncing, danced along the path like a happy child.

Sometimes I wandered alone exploring. The sense of adventure, every corner, caused a halt of breath. And one morning, behind bushes backed by tall trees, I saw a little wooden gate. It was grey-green oak, unpainted, and similar palings surrounded a small neat garden. Behind was a tiny cottage, a gingerbready, witchery house, with arched stone windows. An old man was bent looking at some pink phlox. I watched for a moment gathering courage then, "Good morning," I said.

His head turned sharply sideways, the sun glinting his glasses, then, still bent, he scurried indoors and shut the door.

I told Miranda. She laughed.

"That's old Tom. He was gardener for the man who used to own Mill House. He died and left him the cottage. His father was gardener here before him, and he thinks the place belongs to him. You should hear Rowland! He hates him being there, but what can he do? It's the only fly in the ointment."

"I thought he was bending to look at something, but he walked in still bent."

"Yes. I suppose it's after a lifetime of stooping. He can't

stand up. We hardly ever see him, but very occasionally he fishes from the landing stage which is the only place where Rowland ever fishes, and it infuriates him."

I saw him only once more. He would have been tall and thin but for his disability. His body was almost horizontal with his hips. His hair was silvery-grey and I thought he was a bit like Mr. Montague.

On the first landing was a large room, just as it had been left. Hand in hand we would run, excitedly, up the stairs, and stand, half fearful. Then we would open the door and tiptoe in. The room smelt musty. On the lace runner on the dressing table was a photograph of Mr. Montague as a young man with a girl with a long thin face and frizzy hair and a black velvet band holding a ruff of lace around her throat. A broad thick wedding ring hung on one of the little glass antlers on the frame. Miranda would put it on her finger over her thin one, splay her hand with a comical, head-on-one-side reflective look, then replace it with a grimace. And suddenly we would laugh and fling wide the windows, bursting the cobwebs hung with dead flies, and open the great wardrobe and bring out all the old-fashioned frocks and coats and hats. Lace, satin, mouldy-looking furs—all went on us and round our heads with giggles and screams of laughter.

And in the hall, dark, creepy, was the door leading to that ultimate—absolute—a study. Here, Mr. Montague spent hours and hours with the door locked. But one day Miranda tried the door and said, "Let's peep—"

It was untidy and dusty and books covered three walls.

On the other were photographs of school groups and boat crews and in the corner was a pair of crossed oars. The desk was covered with papers. I had a last breathless look as she closed the door. I felt reverence. It had for me the aura of mystique.

"I must never touch anything," said Miranda.

We ate in the kitchen at the great scrubbed table with the blue checked cloth and one day I watched, through the open door, the sunlight creeping up the pink brick steps. There was boiled chicken with white sauce and a thin pale wine which Mr. Montague had brewed himself. Mr. Montague was at the head of the table, Miranda at the bottom, and I sat at the side and watched Miranda glow behind the big bowl of fruit. She wore her peasant blouse of white muslin. The gathers frilled into an embroidered ruff above the elastic, but below the stuff was stretched taut. Her breasts were heavy, touching the table as she leaned forward, and the nipples showed clearly through the white transparency. It was warm and still and I was flushed, but I drew my cardigan closer over the small swellings that troubled me. Her skin, in the band of sunshine from the window, had a faint veil of down, gossamer wrapping, shielding the blood pulsing in her cheeks, the warm rich ripeness of the nectarine. Not the ones that lay in the bowl, but the living beauties on the wall, warm, soft in the hand, unpicked, bursting with life among the leaves and flowers.

Mr. Montague crumbled bread, and his cultured voice went on and on. I watched the long thin fingers.

He looked round the table.

"We are almost self-supporting. Chickens, the fruit, wine in plenty, vegetables, eggs, milk—" He smiled faintly. "We are almost a citadel. For perfection one must eliminate, cast out anything that is soiled, blemished, simplify, surround oneself, in one's own world, with only the finest of essentials. I have everything I need—"

I held the cool stem of the glass in my hot hand and gazed at the wine as though listening, absorbed, thoughtful. The bowl was lit by the sun from within, a round crystal ball, and when tipped, pictures ran together. The curtains came round Miranda's head and she was a bride, and when she smiled, I tipped it again and the fruit and wine were at her feet. Then I gently tipped it sideways and like a tiny complete picture the table stood upright with all the fruit and flowers still in place and Mr. Montague was pressed underneath and Miranda was leaning over the top laughing, and at the side my own face, elongated, long, white, was watching. Then I held the glass upright and drank the wine in tiny sips. His beautiful voice washed over me in waves. I drowned in his voice. He talked of politics, world affairs—I did not understand what he was saying, but it did not matter. He talked as to someone clever, intelligent, and I was sinking into a dream.

The house had the warmth of meal, of yellow motes that danced in the sunlight that shafted through the circular window on the stairs. Time went on in a golden haze. The house was, to me, always in the heat of the summer.

I never saw it in winter.

* * *

I went again next summer. My heart reached for this fairyland of delight as they stood waiting at the door. It was the same as before—the food, the sunlight, the morning rows up the river. The house was still golden, and all day and in the warmth of the night there was an incessant beat as the calm waters stirred, pulsated, swirled madly, jostled, then rushed towards the fall.

But as the days faded and were lost, not quite the same, Miranda was thinner, her eyes seemed to be searching. One hot day we were sitting, comfortable after the food and wine. Bees droned in the warm thick scent of the honeysuckle by the door, and I was lulled by the beauty of his voice, when Miranda's chair went back with a sharp sound.

"Come on, I can't stand any more of this."

My heart stopped, and from some long deep tunnel in the silence, I saw her half turned, leaning there—she is common, she is common—I watched myself rise and stand, two fingers touching the table like a chairman addressing a meeting.

"I've enjoyed our talk."

I walked after her feeling, This is not real, this is a play. I turned, closing the door, and saw in his eyes pity at my predicament.

Occasionally, now, for the morning row, he changed into white sweater and flannels. He would stand waiting, tall, silvery, like something blanched, as though a young man had been suddenly struck. Instead of ease, he strained at the oars, knuckles white, pointed, above ropy veins, face clenched with a determination, a striving to be rid of this blight.

Then I noticed the man. He stood in the dusk, on the public bank, fishing. He was very tall, dark in the half light and looked unreal in the utter stillness. Every evening Miranda pulled me over the arched rustic bridge to the marshes. She giggled at the man, even touching his coat. She admired the gasping fish and made silly jokes, watching his face. His hands were huge as they gripped the rod, the wrists covered with red-brown hairs. She circled round and round him, her skirts spreading as in a dance. I never heard him speak. He stood tall, dark, mysterious, his cap shading his face.

He became, for me, the embodiment of evil.

But in the bright reality of the day her eyes danced.

"Come and see."

She raced with me up to her room with the old abandon.

"See what my husband has given me for my birthday—"

The earrings hung long and heavy. They weighted her ears, pulling the lobes. They were of dim old silver and diamonds like white opals. Then she pulled down her peasant blouse and we found a ribbon and piled and tied her hair. She caught my hand. "Let's go, let's go along the road to the village, and we'll buy lollipops and pink raspberry drinks, and—"

Mr. Montague was cutting the dead heads from the

roses as we neared on the soft grass. We crept up giggling. Then she touched him suddenly on the arm and swept a curtsey.

"Look!"

She was beautiful, posing there, with her skirt fanned, her eyes bright and questing—like a king's wife in a play. The diamonds trembled and touched her shoulders. He turned, the secateurs in his hand. He half smiled, his eyes cold, indulgent.

"Very nice. But more suitable for a ball."

"What ball?"

An odd discomfort touched me, an embarrassment, as they tensed, as if set for a duel. A look crept over Miranda's face that I had never seen there before, like a hard contemptuous toss of the head, and his eyelids dropped like a blind for protection.

I lay that night watching the moon. It was full, and behind the glass of the window, topped the trees. I watched the dog leaping, or the old man's face. On such a night Dick Turpin rode, and rattled the doors and said, "Who's there!"

The knobbed rail of the bed was a totem post or something seen in a picture of Venice. The faint noise of the fall was like a heart beating. It was the heart of us all, the mill house, the gardens, all of us in the house were gathered round it. It was our heart throbbing and if it stopped, we would shrivel, we would gradually whiten, become dry, transparent and die.

Suddenly, there was another sound. On the landing a

window rattled. I heard the faint drop of the rod that held it open. Pins and needles pricked my head. I slipped my feet out. I saw great headlines, *Young Girl Captures Burglar—Bravery in the Night.* I stood straight, upright, in the frilled nightgown in the long mirror and thought of the young Victoria called from her bed. I drew the thick curtains stealthily to shut out the light and looked at the door. It was tall and heavy and I turned the brass knob.

Miranda stood in the moonlight. Something gauzy from her shoulders touched the floor. She glanced at me vaguely, with acceptance, but did not speak. She watched the white world, leaning forward as though she would spread her arms and gather it to her. Through the trees the drive showed briefly, then vanished. But it went on and joined the road, and that joined other roads, and they swept over moors and dales and through cities. They ran down to the sea and the seas glittered and were touched by other shores and the roads went on through forests, over continents and great crags of mountains.

It all lay there, waiting, in the moonlight.

"If only he had given me a car instead."

Oh, no, not a car, a horse! A great black stallion. I could see it leaping against the moon, with Miranda, with her bare feet, her gipsy skirts and her dark curls flying.

I could not find her the next evening. The house was quiet and the owls in the sitting room looked at me blankly. I went through the dim rooms and corridors then out onto the damp lawn over the bridge and round by the public side. The river ran smoothly, like deep mysterious oil, widening in circles round sudden jewel-hung plops. There was a hush and warm sweaty dampness, and over the marshes the backs of cattle just showed over the low-hung mist. No one was fishing and in the distance the grey metal of the water merged into a great white way, between polled willows like tall pincushions stuck with feathers. Occasionally a cow loomed, a sheet-hung ghost, and the crunch of the gravel was loud under my feet.

And there, by the path, was a black oval mound. I forced my legs on, a wave rose and stuck in my throat. The gravel crunched like gunfire, and then the mound moved. It heaved and parted and I saw two dark bodies and a flash of white thigh. There were low muffled sounds and hotness flamed into my face and something strange rose pounding in my body.

I forced myself on. And when, further along, I crossed the bridge and went back on the soft grass of the private side, I tried not to look as I came level with them again, the river between. I glanced furtively, and the wave burst in my throat, there was movement and a flurry as with low giggling the mound settled again like a dead black rock.

In front of me a faint moon had come up above the great turreted castle of trees, house, and gardens. It made long-reaching shadows, and tipped the water with light. The steps at the side of the boathouse were slimy as I heaved myself up. The scarlet rambler roses by the rail bounced heavy dark red bunches, wet against my hand. The path was muddy, noiseless. I glanced into the boathouse as I went past and there, in the open shed, plain against the silver of the running water, were the man and Miranda.

She hung backwards over his arm like a broken doll. Her full skirt flowed and her blouse was drawn down from naked shoulders. His head and lips were buried, moving savagely over her neck, and on her thrown-back face and closed eyes was a clenched look of agony.

I climbed to the upper terrace and moved numbly, in some nightmare or dream of unreality. From the wall on my left roses hung, limp yellow bells, the stars of the jasmine turned questing to meet me, then twined with the honeysuckle as I passed. At the end of the path, from the open sitting room doors, whitening the lawn and the base of the trees, was a great chute of light.

Mr. Montague sat, the Victorian chair cupping his back, reading. He wore the Norfolk jacket, the rough woollen stockings that I so much admired, and the light from the round white globe lit the silvery head and the deep folds of his neck. I sat just inside the door. He made no sign. The green plush of the chair pricked the back of my legs and the buttons pressed into my back. A tiny gnat, translucent thistledown, danced captive high above the funnel of the oil lamp like a celluloid ball over the jet at a fair.

I watched, entranced, then turned my eyes for relief.

The trees and the house hid the moon and by the clear sharp line of white the yuccas were upturned bayonets round a ghostly chandelier. Beyond was the thick black fur of the night. In its depths was the faint throbbing of the weir, birds rustled with soft sounds and the breath of the jasmine was a drugged drowning sweetness. Its sickliness disturbed me so that for coolness I turned my eyes again.

On the walls of the room photographs of the long-dead shone palely, and the owls watched from their cases. The tall clock was still. There was a hush, a waiting.

Suddenly, noiselessly, Miranda was in the doorway. She swung into the room her black hair rippling, her eyes lit with strange light. She stood in front of him and spread her skirts like the play of a peacock or a half curtsey. Her bare shoulders and neck were covered with bright red marks. Her head was thrown back in vulnerable defiance. He did not raise his eyes or move, and then her head dropped. She did not see me behind the door. I could not speak, and though there was no sound, the room was full of her weeping.

Chapter 3

The next day was quite ordinary. I had expected something dramatic and had been half afraid to come downstairs, but Miranda went about her household duties even cheerfully, and Mr. Montague shut himself into his study and in the evening went off to fish. Before he left, he brought me a large, heavy book. It was enchanting. Fairy tales of butterflies and flowers interspersed with thick vellum tissue-covered pages stuck with specimens of every kind of the bright-winged insects and pressed wild blooms.

"Sit at the table and be very careful with it. Don't carry it about. I did them all as a boy."

He smiled.

"You caught the butterflies and wrote the stories and everything yourself?" I suddenly saw the butterflies brilliant against the hot blue sky then fluttering gently down onto the lavender, the geraniums.

"Yes, I'm afraid so. Fantasies of youth."

I sat all the evening, engrossed, with a warm feeling of pleasure that I should be trusted with it, and importance that he should think I would be interested, and went happily to bed before he came home.

The next morning was my last. I had to be back at school by the following evening. My mother had written frantically "all those things to get ready and pack," but I had begged these few extra hours.

Mr. Montague tapped his brown egg and arranged bread and butter carefully on his plate. His long fingers removed a round of shell with delicate deliberation. Everything was done slowly, with thought behind it. He looked across smiling, first at Miranda and then at me.

"What's it to be this morning? I know"—he held up a hand as I started to speak—"a last row up the river."

"Yes, please."

"Miranda, I am sure, has other plans, so it will be you and I on our own."

Her mouth hardened and a line of brick red streaked her cheeks.

"Yes, I must cook lunch."

"I feel safe with Ann. I always feel that Ann would save me from drowning. Is that not so, Ann?"

"I would do my best."

"Well," he laughed, "let's hope that it won't be necessary. I am just going to the study. Come along there when you are ready."

I helped Miranda clear the table and wash up, then knocked on the study door. He was just closing an envelope as I went in. A basket covered with a napkin stood on the table.

"I wonder if you would do something for me, Ann."

"Yes, of course."

"Would you take this basket and this note to old Tom. I'm afraid that I've been rather unkind to him in the past. One resents the intrusion into one's privacy, you understand. But still—I fear that he often goes hungry. There is just a chicken, a few peaches and plums."

"I'll take them. I won't be long."

"If he's not there, or won't answer the door, you know what he is, just put the letter through the box and leave the basket on the step. I'll be on the landing stage doing a little fishing while I'm waiting."

Miranda stood just outside the half-open door.

"If you're going that way, would you just slip to the shop for me? I've run out of salt," she said.

I felt a flash of annoyance. To run on the soft grass to the cottage was one thing, to go along the hot hard road quite another, on my last day, with Mr. Montague waiting too.

"I suppose so."

She laughed.

"Well, don't look so cross. It won't take long. I can't cook anything without salt."

I knocked and knocked at the door of the cottage, but there was no answer. The place was deadly quiet. So I popped the letter through the slot and stood the basket down. Then I went back to the yellow gravel drive, through the entrance gate and out onto the dusty road.

The little shop stood on its own under a spreading chestnut. Its grey-green thatch fell over like a mat hung out to dry and it seemed almost part of the tree as though the great trunk bulged out at the bottom on one side. Usually I loved the shop. It was dark inside and smelt of paraffin. Fly-spotted yellowing notices had hung for years and there were great glass jars of sweets which had encrusted and stuck at the bottom. It was a post office too, with a separate little counter surrounded by a high wire grid through which old Mrs. Kerrison peered between pamphlets with her shortsighted eyes. I was annoyed this morning. Several old people were waiting, crowding the shop. It was pension day and they leaned on the counter or sat on the two rickety chairs having a chat, in no hurry after their walk from the village, which was quite a long distance away up the road. At last I was next, in front of her—her thin netted hair, her thick round glasses, her high-wired black collar, her bent purple-veined hands resting on the counter.

"Salt, please."

I rushed out clutching the packet. The road looked long, glimmering in the sun. The grounds, the bit of rough wood, the meadows of Mill House, lay behind and encircled the shop. Surely, I thought, there must be a gap. From the entrance gates to where I stood the hedge was thick, clipped, backed by fencing. I wandered up the road towards the village. The hedge grew thin, straggling. I pushed my way through. I was in a meadow and there, at the far end, were the bushes and trees surrounding the cottage. I ran. The back of the cottage was towards me. I pushed open the little gate and was in the vegetable garden with its neatly sticked red-flowered rows of runner beans, onions, marrows ripening, yellow, in the sun. I saw just the top of old Tom's grey head between the little lace kitchen curtains, but I was in a hurry and when I went round the side of the house and out through the front gate, I saw that the basket was gone.

Miranda was not in the kitchen. I plonked the salt on the table, kicked off my shoes and rushed towards the boathouse. I usually chose the lower terrace in daylight. I had been reading a story of someone shut in a cellar and it held for me a morbid fascination. The brick wall on my right was as high as the top of my head. It was surmounted, and the upper terrace thus fenced, with trellis threaded with ramblers. The old stone path was slimy, matted, creepy-cold under my bare feet, the wall grey-green with lichen, roof-lick, snails and an occasional newt. One darted now into the trellis and as I watched it, Miranda swung noiselessly along the upper brick path. I could see the flowered linen hem of her skirt and mud on her strapped sandals as she passed. From her hand hung an awl, gleaming silver, like the dangling skin of a perfectly peeled apple. I did not call, but forgot the newt and hurried. I was late and Mr. Montague did not like waiting. But the landing stage was empty. The boat bobbed gently, tied by its rope, so he had not gone up the river. And then I saw his fishing gear. It was caught in bushes to the right, the rod sticking up, the line with the bright red float draped among the prickles. It was out of my reach. I stood looking down, thinking. The landing stage, built in one with the boathouse and covered by the roof, stretched a good distance out, the edge covering deep water. I always thought it deliciously rickety and dangerous. It was slimy green, and, between cracks and partings in the boards, the water sloshed up, and nearer the bank was squelchy, sticky mud where your bare feet got all dirty and then you went to the edge to wash them, but it was no good, as you had to go back again. I liked looking down through a big wide crack at the black water sucking and swirling underneath where perhaps horrid creatures lurked, big black eels all curled up waiting, or a pike, ready, watching.

But today the landing stage was different. There was no wide crack. It had been repaired, the boards had been moved closer together, and at the back in the dry where the water had not washed them away, were tiny mounds of sawdust.

I wandered back to the house. It was empty. I had to leave in an hour. My packed cases stood in the hall waiting and the taxi was coming at noon. It was too bad. Tears pricked the back of my eyes, and where was Miranda? I went upstairs and washed my legs and feet and put on socks and shoes. I would not call. If they did not want me, I would soon be gone.

I stood in the hall, waiting. The door of the study at the far end was closed. Perhaps he had fallen asleep. I crept towards the door quietly. I tried it gently. It opened. There was no one there. The study looked strangely different—larger, tidier. And then I realized what it was. The papers and some of the books were gone.

I went back to my stand. The round brass pendulum on the grandfather clock swung slowly backwards and forwards, tick tock—tick tock—and then there was a grinding sound as though it gathered all its strength and painfully wrung from its depths came a one—two—three—four—five—six—seven—eight—nine—ten—eleven—twelve—and there was the sound of the taxi on the gravel. I opened the door and the short fat man grunted out and up the steps.

"I'll put these in, miss."

A door burst open and Miranda came flying. Her cheeks were red, her skin damp with sweat.

"Ann! I have been waiting—with food—in the kitchen. You've had nothing. I thought you were rowing."

"I couldn't find Mr. Montague."

"Oh, how awful of him. But you know what he is. Probably wandered off somewhere. He'll be so upset."

"I must be going."

"Well, goodbye, dear. It has been lovely having you. I mean it."

Her arm was round me, her warm damp cheek pressed to mine. I did not move. I stood silently, then, "Can I come again next year?" I said slowly. My heart beat waiting. I thought they liked me. I thought they had wanted me.

Her face went a deeper red and she looked away.

"I may not be here, dear. No, I am sure that I am going away. Perhaps tomorrow, or the next day."

"You are not coming back?"

"No, dear. I am not coming back."

"You are going away with that man—that horrid man?"

"Don't say that. You don't understand."

"You are leaving Mr. Montague all alone."

I turned to the door where, down the steps, the taxi chugged and the fat man stood waiting.

"Ann"—she held me by the arm—"when you are older, you will remember and understand. Now you don't understand these things."

I looked from the back window. She stood on the top step by the open door and put up her hand, but I did not wave back.

Chapter 4

The school was a converted Victorian house at the end of a dark drive lined with cypresses. Grey clouds drifted slowly across the tall windows of the music room.

"Come along. Three-four time."

"My hands are cold."

"So are mine. We must expect that in November." Miss Mattocks rubbed the fingers at the end of her black mittens. "They will soon warm up when you get going."

I sat looking at the sheet of music before me. I was good at Theory. I got high marks for Theory. I could sit alone with my own thoughts and work it out. Now I sat still and quiet, my eyes going forward reading the notes, and suddenly—I saw—I heard the music roll, the waves crashing, the call of the gull.

"Come along," said Miss Mattocks. "No time for dreaming—three—four," and it was just Miss Mattocks, her fuzzy hair, the jet on her mittens, my cold hands, the tick tock of the metronome. It was just the music lesson.

"Pedal up, pedal down," said Miss Mattocks, "so important with these classical pieces."

"How did you get on with old Matty today?" Iris Baltrop edged up to me as I came out into the corridor.

"Not so bad. I got through it anyway."

She looked round and then put her face close to mine. I looked quickly at the dark greasy hair, the pointed sallow face, then away. Her breath smelt.

"You can have it first tonight. I've got it here, tied up."

She tapped her gym slip at the waist. I saw the paper lying on her skin, pungent, damp.

Miss Knight was coming down the corridor.

"Don't forget," Iris whispered, "you can have it first tonight."

"Come along, girls." Miss Knight swept us forward with an imaginary hand, "suppertime. We don't want everything to get cold, do we?"

Iris Baltrop was a weekly boarder. Her parents had the butcher's shop in the village where we lived. My mother said they were common. She was determined that I should be a full boarder so that I should have nice friends and not mix up with the village folk. It made a girl different, she said, to be a boarder at a good school. It taught her to speak and behave nicely. Olive Winter was a full boarder. Her people were corn merchants and millers. Her father was a magistrate and they lived in a big stone house.

"There's a nice friend for you," Mother would say wistfully.

After each weekend Iris Baltrop brought back the Sunday paper. She brought it secretly strapped somewhere on her person. It was a paper that my mother would not have in the house. Iris kept the paper hidden until Monday night, savouring her power. No one knew who would be her favourite. Sometimes one girl had the whole paper in a lighted cavern under the bedclothes, and sometimes sheets were distributed and passed quickly round. These were the best times, with lighted igloos glowing and giggles and naughty bits read out in horror-stricken excited voices. Iris's power waned about Wednesday, had sunk to a dead low on Thursday, then rose slowly and reached a sharp crescendo on Friday afternoons when she was driven away by her powdered mother.

Now she sat opposite to me across the long narrow table. Her eyes, as brown and small as a bird's, watched me eat. She seemed to stop and stare every time I looked up. The small piece of cod in the grey sticky sauce merged into the pale green of the beans that had been warmed up for three days. Why did she sit so quietly and stare? She was usually at the far end of the table jabbering and laughing. I glanced up quickly to catch her out and she was looking at me intently, her sharp nose pointed forward, as though I was something she had found.

"Baked apples, again!" she said.

Miss Knight's chair scraped back. We rose and folded our hands.

"Thank the Lord."

Olive Winter was coming down the room importantly.

She was tall, fair-haired, pink-cheeked and composed. She was a prefect and a year older than I.

"Miss Knight wants to see you in her study immediately."

Iris's eyes suddenly blazed with excitement. She went crimson. She grimaced at Olive's back.

"Stuck-up ass! Why do you think Old Knight Errant wants to see you?"

"I don't know. I can't think of anything."

"Tell me about it when you come out. Don't forget you can have the paper tonight."

She went with me to the study door. She linked her arm in mine and her hipbone jogged against my thigh as we walked.

"I'll knock," she whispered.

"Come in," called a voice.

Iris slipped to the side and flattened against the wall. I closed the door firmly, giving it an extra push to make sure that it was shut. Miss Knight sat behind her desk. There was a fire in the grate and the curtains were drawn. She quickly stubbed out a cigarette.

"Well, you can sit down. Don't look so scared. You haven't been robbing a bank, have you?"

She laughed. She was in her jolly mood. Her grey-streaked, coarse, bobbed hair put back with a brown slide stood out at the ends in front of the light behind. Her tweed suit fitted squarely. Her blouse collar looked white below the ruddy neck. Her large hands played with the ruler in front of her.

"Now why do you think I have sent for you?"

"I don't know."

"I don't know—what?"

"I don't know, Miss Knight."

"Well, it's nothing bad this time. No, Miss Mattocks says that you are trying harder. No, it's nothing like that. The fact is I've had a letter from your mother. She seems to think that it would be better if you stayed at school for half term."

My heart beat. I stared at the hairs on her chin. Stay at school for half term! We lived only five miles away. The only girls who did not go home for half term were Sonia, whose parents were in India, Patsy the coloured girl, and May Thompson, who was an orphan. Stay at school during a holiday! My mother did not want me. Tears pricked my eyes. The blood came burning to my face. I looked up. Miss Knight was still, watching me. Her eyes had the same expression that I had seen in Iris Baltrop's—excitement, tense, as though there was something strange about me. She blinked—and it was gone. I would not cry in front of her. I felt suddenly alone.

"Did she say why?"

"She is writing to explain to you. There is something going on and she thinks that you are best out of it. You will understand later."

I looked at her and she got up briskly.

"Well, that's that. Now run along and don't brood. Have a good sleep and get on with your work. It will all come right in the end."

I walked to the door.

"Good night, Miss Knight."

"Good night, Ann. And don't say anything to the others."

They were in the common room. All the girls grouped in a ring round Iris Baltrop. The noise stopped as I opened the door and they looked up. Their faces were flushed, excited, and in their eyes was the same expression that I had just seen in Miss Knight's.

"What did she say?"

"Nothing much."

"It must have been something."

"Just about the music."

"Oh."

They seemed disappointed. They seemed to flatten.

"Let's go to bed." Iris jumped up and gathered some books. "Let's go to bed and read."

Everyone sprang around chattering.

"But there's another half hour yet. It's only half-past seven."

"Oh, come on. There's nothing to do. It'll please old Mattie. She can be quiet for once. Come on, we can read for half an hour before lights out."

The ten girls in our dorm pressed the door shut against the others.

"We don't want you! Go to your own beds!"

"Now then, girls, what's all this!"

Miss Fletcher was on the landing.

"We're going to bed early, Miss Fletcher. We thought we would read until lights out."

"Well, that's all right. Yes—that's a good idea. Have you some good books?"

"Yes, Miss Fletcher, we got some history books from the library."

"Well"—she shooed the others—"go quietly and settle down. Have you all cleaned your teeth?"

"Yes, Miss Fletcher."

"Well, good night, all. Someone will be round in half an hour."

I undressed slowly. I was last into bed. They were all sitting up watching me. I lifted my legs and slipped in between the sheets. Like a flash Iris was across to me.

"Here's the paper."

It was in a tight small wad. Iris went back to her bed, looking over her shoulder. I opened it out. The lines, the folds, made small squares. I sat looking at the front page. A feeling of strangeness, of fear, vague, cold, tightened my throat. They were all watching. No one was reading. They sat up in bed, their eyes on me. I glanced down at the small print. I was not really interested. I could feel Iris waiting, impatient, like something ready to pounce. Why had she given me the paper? She had never done so before; only twice had I even had one sheet to read. Why didn't the others mind—usually there was quarrelling and pulling, shouts of "Let me have it." "Let me, you promised." Now they were quiet, watching. I shut my eyes to hide the tears;

it was as though they were in a ring closing, closing.

"Why don't you read it? Don't you want it?"

I opened my eyes and studied the front page intently.

"Why don't you turn over? You've read that."

I did not speak.

Iris Baltrop was beside me. She lay on the bed, her damp acrid arm around my neck.

"Turn it over. Don't you want to? You've finished that."

She seized the bottom corner with her left hand and flicked it towards her. On the third page was a large picture of Miranda.

"She's your cousin, isn't she?"

They all rose in their white gowns and settled round my bed like a flock of geese, squawking.

"She's murdered her husband!"

"You were staying there, weren't you?"

"You'll have to go as a witness!"

"My mother says you'll be the chief witness."

They all stopped and looked at Iris Baltrop.

"My mother says you're the only one who knew anything about it."

"You'll have to go to court!" They all screeched.

"My mother says she was carrying on with some man."

Eyes rounded and they moved closer to Iris.

"Yes, my mother says she was carrying on with Jeff Mitchell."

"Who was he? Where did he live?"

"Mrs. Goodrum, who did for him, comes to help my mother twice a week and she told her all about it."

"Tell us, tell us."

They pressed around Iris, sitting on my bed.

"He lived in a cottage on Shepherd's farm. He'd come from Australia and he was looking round for a farm of his own. But he kept telling Mrs. Goodrum they were too expensive. He said he hadn't enough money to buy the farm, the horses and the stock and all. He said he thought of going back."

"Did he say anything about Mrs. Montague?" Barbara Day's eyes stuck out, her face went red, her voice was a hoarse whisper.

"Had she seen them carrying on?"

"He told Mrs. Goodrum she was a rare nice woman, and if she'd been free he'd have married her, and she said she said, 'Her husband's an old man. There's a lot of money there. You might not have long to wait,' and he laughed and laughed and said the tough old boy would live for ever, and something about he didn't want dead men's shoes."

"What does that mean?"

"I don't know. Go on, Iris; hurry up, Iris. What else did she say?"

"On the Friday, the day of the murder, he gave Mrs. Goodrum extra money and said he wouldn't want her any more. He said he was leaving that morning. He said nobody would miss him, the English were an unfriendly lot, and the only person he knew well besides Mrs. Goodrum was Mrs. Montague, and he'd said goodbye to her the night before."

I suddenly saw her hanging over his arm—in the moonlight—in the silver light.

The door opened. Miss Fletcher was in the room.

"Come along, all in bed, lights out, it's well past eight."

They scampered away.

"What were you doing all around poor Ann?"

"Just talking, Miss Fletcher."

I had forgotten the paper, but she did not seem to notice. One of the girls at the far end saw it.

"I've got something growing on my neck, Miss Fletcher. It hurts, Miss Fletcher."

"Lift up your hair and let me see."

I pushed the paper down near my feet.

"It's only a pimple. A little Zambuck and it will go."

"Yes, Miss Fletcher. Thank you, Miss Fletcher."

It was dark and quiet. I stared into the blackness.

"What will you wear?" said a hoarse whisper.

I woke in the night. The paper perhaps woke me. It made a harsh crackle when I moved my legs. I lit my torch under the bedclothes and drew it gently up. I read the small print under the picture.

> Mrs. Miranda Montague, widow of the deceased.
>
> The inquest held on Saturday on the death of Mr. Rowland Montague of the Mill House, Little Snelling, Suffolk, was adjourned.

Chapter 5

They came to get me on a cold wet afternoon before the Christmas holidays. Miss Knight summoned me to her study in the morning and prepared me for this outing. She sat as usual behind the desk with the big fire burning in the grate and the cigarette smoke still hovering.

"Now there is nothing to worry about. This is the magistrate's court, just a preliminary hearing. I shall be coming with you, and your mother will be in the car when it arrives. Have you cleaned your shoes and got a fresh hanky?"

"Yes, Miss Knight."

"Just tell the truth. Just say what you saw and what you heard; you can't go very wrong on that. They will ask you questions, and all you have to do is give the answers."

"Yes, Miss Knight."

"Well, run along and be waiting near the front door at one-thirty, not a minute later. I should brush out your hair and braid it again and see that your nails are clean. You are let off lessons for the rest of the day."

"Thank you, Miss Knight."

There was a moment's silence. A log that had been suspended by another partially charred fell into place. There was a spatter of red sparks, then it burned up brightly. She looked down at the desk and fiddled with a ruler.

"Did you"—her face flushed slightly, she did not look up—"see them—kissing or anything?"

Something tightened in my chest. A wall suddenly rose between—as though I had been asked to show a private part to a stranger in a public place.

"No, Miss Knight."

She still looked down.

"You may go."

We waited on black leather seats in a long corridor. Two men were sitting one on each side of me with my mother at one end and Miss Knight at the other. Policemen strolled past and young men hurried, carrying sheaves of paper.

"Call Ann Fielding. Call Ann Fielding!"

The men rose, one held my hand.

"Come along."

The door through which I had seen the young men hurrying opened and we walked in. It was a large brown room with high windows. I went up two steps into a kind of box. Mrs. Kerrison, strange in a round black hat with a rusty feather, was just stepping down.

I stood alone, my hands resting on the broad ledge in front of me. My mother and Miss Knight sat on the chairs with four or five other people and right across, on the other side, was Miranda. She looked different. I never realized that she had such high cheekbones or that her eyes were so large. She was pale, but this was winter and I had only seen her brown and blooming in summer. She stared at me and suddenly her eyes filled with tears.

A man was hurrying across with an open book in his hand. He laid it facing me on the ledge. It was the Bible.

"Raise your right hand and say after me, 'I swear by Almighty God that the evidence I shall give shall be the truth, the whole truth, and nothing but the truth.' "

I looked at my mother. Her set face bent painfully into a slight smile and she nodded.

"I swear—by Almighty God—that the evidence I shall give shall be the truth, the whole truth—and nothing but the truth."

He shut the book with a bang and took it over to a table behind which three people were sitting. One was a woman wearing a hat and in the centre was a grey-haired man writing. He looked up, took off his glasses and smiled at me.

"You are Ann Fielding, aged fourteen years, of—" he put on his spectacles and glanced down—"Kiln Farm, Bampton, and currently at school at Walton House School for Girls, Walton."

"Yes, sir."

"You are a cousin of the accused, Mrs. Miranda Montague."

"Yes, sir."

"You spent part of your summer holiday in the years nineteen twenty-five and nineteen twenty-six with your cousin and her husband at the Mill House, Little Snelling?"

"Yes, sir."

He removed his spectacles and smiled, settling back in the chair.

"What did you think of Mr. Montague, or did you call him by his Christian name?"

"I called him Mr. Montague. I thought he was a nice gentleman."

"Did he and your cousin, his wife, get on together? I mean did they have any quarrels or disagreements?"

"They didn't the first time I was there."

"Oh—you mean that they did during the next holiday—which would be this year."

"Well—"

"Did they or did they not?"

"Well—it didn't seem the same—"

"You mean the atmosphere was different?"

"Yes, it didn't seem the same."

"Do you think now that there were possibly disagreements when you were not there and they caused this feeling that you had?"

"I don't know."

"In what way was it different?" His eyes stared into

mine. It was as though I was caught at the end of a line, he at one end and I the other. But I dare not look away. He was holding me safely on the line. I could just answer the questions. The people were a blur of colour.

"She did not like him talking."

"He talked a lot?"

"Yes."

"When?"

"At mealtimes."

"What about?"

"Oh, all sorts of things, the government—foreign countries—and— Oh, all sorts of things."

"He was a clever man?"

"Yes."

"You liked him?"

"Yes, I did."

"He had received a better education, perhaps, than your cousin—"

"Yes, I think he had."

"Was she ever rude to him in front of you?"

"Yes, once."

"What did she say?"

"She got up and said she'd had enough of it."

A slight murmuring quickly died.

"Tell me exactly what happened on the last morning of your stay, on the morning that Mr. Montague was drowned."

"Well, we were having breakfast and he asked me what I would like to do on my last morning and I said a row up the river, and he said come to the study when I was ready and we would go."

"And this you did?"

"Yes, but when I went, he asked me to take a basket of things and a note to old Tom, the gardener. I said I would and then Miranda asked me to get some salt from the village shop."

"The village shop was quite a way?"

"Well, it's not too far, but I felt a bit cross, as I thought there wouldn't be time for much of a row."

"But you said you would?"

"Yes, and Mr. Montague said he would be fishing on the landing stage while he was waiting."

"Tell me what you did then."

"I knocked at Tom's door but couldn't make him hear, so I left the basket on the step and put the note through the letter box and when I got to the shop, it was pension morning so I had to wait."

"A number of old people were there?"

"Yes, but I got served and went back by a short cut. The basket was gone, so Tom had taken it in."

"Then you went straight to the landing stage?"

"No, I went into the house to put the salt in the kitchen and take off my shoes. I did not want them to get wet and dirty as I had to wear them to go home. Then I went by the lower terrace to the landing stage."

"Was your cousin, Miranda, in the house, did you see her at all?"

"She wasn't in the house, but as I ran along the bottom terrace, she was going back to the house. She didn't see me, and as I was in a hurry, I didn't call. I could just see her legs and skirt."

"You saw her feet?"

"Yes, she had sandals on."

"Were they muddy?"

"Yes."

"And that is all?"

"She was carrying something."

"What was that?"

"An awl."

"You know what an awl is?"

"Yes, I have seen my father using one."

"Go on, you went to the landing stage?"

"But he wasn't there."

"Did you see anything? Anything different, or lying about?"

"His fishing rod was tangled in some bushes."

"Where were these bushes, to the right or the left?"

"To the right, and the landing stage was different."

"Oh—" he looked at me sharply, as though he had known the answers to the other questions, but this was new.

"How was it different?"

"Well, the boards were closer together."

"There was no new wood as though the stage had been repaired, they were just closer together—"

"Yes, there had been some gaps and I—" I felt a flush hot on my cheeks—"I used to watch the water slopping up from underneath."

He smiled.

"The sort of thing I did when I was a boy. But now you mean that there were no gaps, they were closer together?"

"Not all of them. Just two where there had been a big wide gap."

"Nearer to the water or the bank?"

"Nearer to the water, about two planks back from the river."

"Did you notice anything else?"

"There were little piles of sawdust."

"This was dry?"

"Yes, it was right at the back, near the ground."

"Yes, thank you. Well, now we come to another matter. Did you ever see your cousin, Miranda, with a man?"

"Yes."

"How often?"

"Several times."

"She used to meet him?"

"Yes."

"Did he ever come to the house? Was he a friend of the family?"

"No."

"How did you see them? Did you come across them accidentally?"

"No, I used to go with her round by the river."

"Round by the river?"

"Round by the public side."

"Did she, do you think, want you with her?"

"She asked me to go, she said Mr. Montague would not mind if I was with her, she said he liked me, he—" I broke from his eyes; I put my head down; my hands looked distorted through a swim of tears—"trusted me."

"Yes, my dear, don't distress yourself. You are doing very well. Did you like this man?"

"I never spoke to him."

"Did you talk about him to your cousin?"

"Only once or twice."

"What did she say?"

"She said he was—young."

"Meaning perhaps that her husband was old. Did her manner of speaking imply that?"

"Yes."

"Did you ever, now think slowly and carefully, did you ever see anything that would make you think that they were more than friends? Did you ever see them with—his arms around her, did you ever see them—kissing?"

There was silence. A sort of hush, a waiting—then a soft voice in the court said, "Shame!" I glanced up. My mother, her face was white, frozen, her eyes down. Miss Knight was composed, wearing a look of slight disappointment. Miranda—Miranda's hands were clenched on the rail in front. Her black eyes were fastened on mine, wide, beseeching.

"Take your time, there is no hurry."

—The moonlight—in the silver light—I swear by Almighty God—the truth—and nothing but the truth—I turned my face from Miranda—

"Yes."

Miss Knight was looking straight at me. Rage flashed, ripped for a second across her eyes, and was gone, leaving blankness.

Chapter 6

"She's been arrested!"

Iris Baltrop's voice screeched in the little room that was called the library.

"She was before, but now she is properly. She's in Holloway Jail!" The girls packed, pressing round her flushed important figure.

"I know where she is because she wrote to Mrs. Goodrum and asked her to go and see her and take her some things!"

Miranda—would my mother, her only relative, go to see her—Miranda?

The door opened.

"Come along, girls. What's all the noise? The library's for quiet reading, not uproar. Get on with your prep. Ann, it's time for your music lesson."

Pedal up—pedal down—pedal up—pedal down—tick tock—tick tock. I shut my eyes and saw the pendulum in the hall swinging backwards and forwards, backwards and forwards.

"Now come along, wake up and take an interest in what you are doing. Three-four time. Wrists up, pedal down, crescendo there, now slower, slower."

"Yes, Miss Mattocks—"

I rose and folded my music books. I was stiff with cold. I turned to the door. There was a slight scratch of wool and jet on my hand.

"I know what you're going through, dear"—her little eyes blinked behind the glasses—"but believe me, it's best to keep up with the ordinary things."

"Yes, thank you, Miss Mattocks."

"Don't talk about it too much to the others, especially—" she hesitated, but I knew who she meant. "You're different, dear. Remember what I say."

"Yes, Miss Mattocks."

Iris was waiting. She was my lieutenant. She had taken charge of me. I had been raised to the rank of goddess in the school. Girls hung on my every word, rushed to do my bidding, boasted that they knew me, that they had touched my hand or fetched my book. It was exciting, exhilarating. It was taken for granted that I had the paper first. Even privacy was arranged. In the garden was a small forsaken lavatory, an amenity before the sewers had been put in. This had been cleaned and brushed by excited slaves, a strip of old carpet put on the lid and here I was ushered, paper in hand, as soon as possible on a Monday, while Iris stood outside, the others packed around, like a general briefing soldiers for a battle.

"Of course she wants to read it by herself. In private. Without all you lot looking on. It's only natural."

Miss Knight avoided contact with a blank stare. Only once did she lose control. She came across me in the centre of a little group and pulled me out roughly, hurting my arm.

"Get on with your work. Upsetting the school. We want no prima donnas here."

For weeks there was nothing in the paper, and then, on one cold bright April Monday morning, Iris came back furious.

"My mother's lent the paper to Mrs. Goodrum. But it's in! The trial's at the next assizes! Next week! My mother's ordered six Sunday papers to lend out, so we're sure to get one—and my mother's going to the trial! She's going to stay with my aunt for the whole time and they're going to get there at about three in the morning and take rugs and coffee every day to make sure they get in. And my mother says have you got a photograph or will you have one taken and will you sign it 'To Iris with love from Ann' because she wants to send it with the paper to Canada to her cousin's and you're my best friend— What will you wear? My mother says you want something smart, she says she'll go with you and me to a shop and choose something if you like. She says it's nearly summer and yellow would be nice and she says you should wear a little rouge and a touch of lipstick because you're so pale. She says your photograph will be in all the papers and go all over the world, so you want to look nice—"

Faces hung, pale, mouths open, mesmerized—

"And on the day that you go up to the trial, my mother's going to tell them that you are at her daughter's school and that you're my best friend and that you come from our village, and it would help if you could see her, and would they give her a better place—my mother says . . ."

I went home for the Easter holiday. My mother sat silent stitching a white collar onto my navy alpaca. And on April the 28th, early in the morning, a car, with two men, came for me and my mother and father.

Chapter 7

A garden of moondaisies waited. Faces turned, uplifted to mine. The box in which I was standing was similar to the one before, but higher, larger, and more solid. To my right, level with me, in a great high-backed chair against oak panelling sat an old man in a curled white wig. I looked over the blur of faces below. At a table writing were other men in white wigs and opposite, again raised level with me, were three rows of people behind dark wood on which their hands rested. Right at the back, against the opposite wall to the old man, stood Miranda. Her hair was cut short to just below the ears. Her neck, without the bouncing curls, looked long and thin. I looked across the hall into her eyes and felt mine fill, and dampness on my cheeks. She smiled, a tiny movement of her white face, and shook her head.

A man came as before and laid the Bible before me.

"Face the judge," he whispered, and looked towards the

old man, "and call him my lord if he addresses you." He raised his voice. "Now say after me, 'I swear . . .' "

One of the men sitting at the table rose and came towards me.

"You are Ann Fielding of . . ."

"Yes, sir."

"You stayed with . . ."

I felt like a parrot answering the questions as they rolled on. They were exactly the same as I had answered before—"Yes, sir." "No, sir." It was so easy. Even the judge's eyes were closed over his thin beak of a nose, his head slightly nodding. "I couldn't make old Tom hear, so I put the note in the letter box and the basket on the step—"

The judge's eyes suddenly opened. He rapped the desk in front of him with a knobbed ruler. It made me jump, my heart suddenly beating.

"Why hasn't this witness been called?"

"He is deaf, nearly blind, illiterate, my lord, his mind is wandering, he is suffering from senile decay. But we have the letter, my lord. You will hear from the next witness, my lord, a Mrs. Kerrison, how he took the letter to her to decipher."

The old man settled back and closed his eyes.

"Carry on, Mr. Cameron."

"Thank you, my lord."

The man turned again to me.

"What happened then?"

"I had to wait because it was pension day and there were a lot of old people in the shop."

"Did your cousin know it was pension day? Had she ever mentioned it to you before? How did you know it was pension day, that it was why the old people were there?"

"She had sometimes laughed and said, 'Oh, it's no good going down there this morning, you'd never get away. Better wait until this afternoon.' "

"Do you think that she deliberately sent you there to get you out of the way?"

"I don't know."

"When did she tell you to go? Where was she when her husband asked you to take the basket and the note to Tom?"

"She was just outside the study door."

"It was open?"

"Yes."

"She was listening?"

"She might have been."

"When you left the shop, what did you do?"

"I saw a gap and thought it would be a short cut, so I pushed my way through, and I had to go across old Tom's garden to get to the Mill House."

"You went into the garden at the back of the cottage?"

"Yes."

"The vegetable garden?"

"Yes, and I went round by the side of the cottage into the flower garden at the front and out of the gate and the basket had gone."

"Did you see Tom at all this second time?"

"Yes."

"To speak to?"

"No, I just saw him through the window."

"The back window?"

"Yes, from the vegetable garden. If the basket was still on the front step, I was going back to tell him, but as it had gone, I thought it was all right."

"Yes, go on."

"I went into the kitchen to give Miranda the salt, but she wasn't there so I put it down—"

"Yes, go on."

The blood flooded into my face. As I had been speaking, pictures had opened before my eyes—the shop—the gap—the back garden—the cottage—the front garden—running across the grass—the lawn—the rose bushes—the back door—the kitchen—the kitchen—the brick floor, the large scrubbed dresser, the rows of canisters, tea, rice, sugar, salt—on the dresser had been a large just-opened packet of salt. A memory floated up of the day before when I had helped peel the potatoes, of lifting down this heavy packet, sprinkling salt into the saucepan and putting it back.

"Go on. Do you feel faint?"

"No, I've just remembered something."

There was deep quiet, a tenseness.

"There was a packet of salt on the dresser."

"You put down the packet of salt that you had just bought and there was another one on the dresser?"

"Yes."

"Perhaps your cousin required two packets."

"No, she said she hadn't any, and she couldn't cook anything without salt."

A kind of Oh! went round the court like a ripple.

"Silence!" The judge rapped his hammer. "Proceed, Mr. Cameron."

"What did you do then?"

"I took my shoes off and ran towards the landing stage by the lower terrace and I saw my cousin walking along the upper terrace. I could just see her skirt and her feet and legs."

"Why couldn't you see all of her?"

"There is a fence of trellis with rambler roses. The roses were thick at the top, but thin, just branches, at the bottom."

"Did she see you?"

"No."

"Were her shoes muddy?"

"Yes and she was carrying an awl."

"An awl?"

"A long twisted thing that you drill holes with."

I was beginning to feel quite expert. I knew what the next questions would be, so I answered them before they were asked.

"Yes, go on."

"When I got to the landing stage, Mr. Montague was not there. His fishing rod was laying over the bushes."

"Where exactly was his fishing rod?"

"There are some bushes on the right-hand side jutting out over the water and I noticed it because the red float was sticking up. The line was just sort of draped, tangled over the top."

"Did you try to get it, to recover it?"

"I couldn't reach it."

"So no one could have laid it there. It must have been thrown?"

"Yes, I suppose so."

"If someone had been pushed into the water while fishing, or sitting with it in his hands and thrown up his arms, it would land just there?"

"It might have done."

"This is a case for the experts, not this young child, Mr. Cameron!"

"Yes, my lord; I'm sorry, my lord."

"Carry on, Mr. Cameron."

"Did you notice anything else?"

"Yes, the planks had been put closer together."

"Put closer together?"

"Yes, there were no gaps. There had been gaps where you could see the water."

"Did you notice anything else?"

"Yes, little piles of sawdust, in the dry, nearer the bank."

"Was this sawdust from old wood or new wood? Was it yellow?"

"Yes."

"So if someone had been standing near the bank and putting holes into new wood ready for nails, this is how the little piles of sawdust would look?"

"Yes."

"What did you do then?"

"I went back to the house."

"Did you see anyone?"

"No, there was no one there. I went into the kitchen and all the downstairs rooms and then I went upstairs to wash."

"And you saw no one? There was no one in the house? What did you do then?"

"I waited in the hall and the taxi came. And then Miranda came rushing towards me."

"You say—rushing. Was she agitated? Flushed? As though she had been hurrying?"

"Yes, she was."

"What did she say?"

"She said she had been waiting with food in the kitchen."

"But you had looked in the kitchen."

"Yes, she was not there."

"What else did she say?"

"She said that Mr. Montague had probably wandered off somewhere."

"The taxi was waiting?"

"Yes."

"So that was all? You said goodbye?"

"I asked her if I could stay again next year."

"And what did she say?"

"She said she wouldn't be there."

"She said that she was going away?"

"Yes."

"When?"

"She said perhaps tomorrow or the next day. She said she was not coming back."

"What did you say then?"

I flushed, waited. A sudden shyness gripped me—all those people listening. I did not look at them but they were there, at the side, the lines of men in front of me, all watching; I swallowed, the judge sat up there in his white wig just like God, I swear by Almighty God—

"I said, 'You are going away with that horrid man.' "

A wave like a sigh went over the court.

"I said, 'You are leaving Mr. Montague all alone.' "

"What did she say?"

"She said when I was older I would understand. She said that now I didn't understand these things."

"What horrid man was this?"

I wished I hadn't said it, I wished—

"Who was this man?"

"A man Miranda was friendly with."

"Friendly? How friendly? Did he come to the house? Was he a friend of her husband's?"

"No, she met him by the river."

"How often did she meet him? Every night?"

"I don't know."

"Why did you call him 'this horrid man'? Didn't you like him? What didn't you like about it if he was just a friend?"

"Miranda used to ask me to go with her. She said Mr. Montague wouldn't suspect if I was with her."

"Suspect? What was there to suspect if he was just a friend? Did you see anything to make you think that he was more than that?"

I did not answer.

"Did you ever see them kissing? Did you see her in a state of deshabille?"

Deshabille? What was that? The marks on her throat? Her blouse pulled down?

"Yes."

He turned, made a slight bending movement to the judge, and sat down. Another man in a white wig approached.

"You saw the gardener through the window on your way back from the shop."

"Yes."

"Tell me exactly what you saw."

"I just saw the top of his head."

"The front or the back?"

"The back."

"By the height of the head, he was sitting, do you think?"

"Yes, he was sitting by the window."

"Did you see the head move?"

"Yes, it vanished for a second as though he was picking something up and then came back again."

"Thank you."

*   *   *

We went, my mother, my father and I to a small dark room. They brought us sandwiches and a pot of tea and put them down on one end of the long heavy table. A young policeman stood just inside the door. He had his hands behind his back and shifted occasionally from one foot to the other. Outside, behind the small frosted window, there was a dull roar like the sound of the weir. But this roar was not steady. It did not keep on one note. It surged like a wave and then died and then rose again. There were sharp staccato peaks, whistles and laughter. Sometimes a long-drawn-out "Oh!"

I went to the lavatory. My mother came with me. Our policeman spoke to another standing just outside the room and he followed us and stood in the corridor with his back to the door.

They brought us another pot of tea and a plate of cakes. And then, when the window was pearl-grey and the lights were lit, one of the men who had ridden with us came in. Our policeman pulled himself up and saluted.

"Join the squad."

"Yes, sir."

"She's just going from the back. Get Perkins and draw as much attention as possible to the front."

"Yes, sir."

"Keep steady. No breaks. At all costs, no breaks."

"No, sir."

"They're ugly. Keep attention at the front."

He turned to us.

"She won't be called again now. They've adjourned. We'll be going. Now, young lady"—he took my hand, shook it, and smiled—"you've done very well. Just a little more of your bravery and you'll be out of it and home for good. When you go out of that entrance, keep your head down while you walk the few steps to the car. Don't look round, there's nothing to be frightened of. Come now"—he pulled my open coat up on the shoulders, put my plaits inside and pulled the brim of my hat down.

"Button it up, it's cold." He turned to my father.

"Ready, sir? We'll be going."

Two policemen opened the great doors from the centre. I stood on the top of the flight of stone steps. A huge sea of people, a grey blanket, heaved and moved. It was again the rats; the council rubbish dump at the far end of our farm, there were sometimes ornaments; broken toys, and one night in the dusk the whole thing had moved, a grey blanket, it was rats, the old nightmare—the old terror.

A great scream screeched into the air.

"It's her!"

A booing rumbled like waves of thunder.

"No, it ain't! It's the kid!"

"They've tricked us! Round by the back!"

Pieces broke off and rushed away. I walked down the steps between lines of linked police, the man's grip iron-hard on my arm. I was in the car. We started to move like a ship churning through sea.

"That's right, dearie." A woman tapped the glass. "You tell um, you tell um all you know—the Jezebel!"

I was home. The man stayed for a while talking downstairs with my mother and father, then I heard the car start, saw the lights sweep the drive and he was gone.

Chapter 8

It was a relief to be back at school. For the remaining three days of the holiday there had been almost complete silence. No word except "Come to dinner"—"Go to bed"—passed my mother's lips. On the last two mornings the postman had brought a long sealed envelope, the contents of which my mother and father read without passing to me. No papers were delivered, no news came.

Iris, the girls—and the papers—seemed like a wave of gaiety. Iris staggered under a stack of back numbers and the words "My mother said" were a constant jingle, a lilt, in my head. The air was warmer, the daffodils were pushing through the damp turf, and, round by the old lavatory, the bushes were thickening with leaves.

The papers were kept in this cubbyhole and one of the girls, currying favour, had brought a small padlock so that, with this outside and the bolt within, it became a doubly fortified fortress. There were all the daily papers as well as one for each week, and the whole undertaking was organized by Iris. One for each day containing news of the trial was laid on the carpeted seat, and the surplus was distributed to her favourities to be secreted on their persons, or in their lockers, to be read at night.

Our recreation periods in the grounds were longer now that the evenings were lighter and in the warm dark box I read my first news. On the front page were photographs —a large one of Miranda, the same that I had seen in the paper before. It had stood in a silver frame in the sitting room at the Mill House. There was Mrs. Kerrison in her black hat—and me. I stood on the top of the steps with the crowd around. I looked funny with my collar up, no hair, and my hat pulled down. I read snatches in the dim light.

The trial opened before the Rt. Hon. Lord Justice Harold. Crowds, mostly women, had waited wrapped in rugs, one even with a camp bed, through the cold wet night. One woman said that since she was sixteen, she had been at every murder trial in the country and had never let anything stop her. The courtroom, packed to capacity, held only a small proportion of the throng that surged to the entrance waiting to get in. The accused, a dark-haired, dark-eyed girl, just twenty-two years old, of a surprising beauty, was calm throughout the first day. She answered the charge with a firm "Not guilty." She appeared to have a feeling of expectancy as though the trial was something to be got through, but that it would clear the matter up. Her eyes flickered to each witness for the prosecution with detachment. Only when the young girl Ann Fielding took the stand did she come to life. This, one felt, was what she had been waiting for. She blossomed and smiled reassuringly at the girl. Only at the end of this witness's evidence did her face whiten and her lips tremble.

The first witness examined by Mr. Arnold Cameron, KC, for the prosecution was a Mr. Hatcher, a bright young fellow with ginger hair.

Mr. Cameron: "You are a timber merchant residing in the village of Little Snelling?"

"Yes, sir."

"On September the twenty-fifth, nineteen twenty-six, you received a telephone call from Mrs. Montague ordering two lengths of wood."

"Yes, sir."

"Did she give definite instructions as to the size?"

"Yes, sir, five feet in length."

"It was a very small order? Had you ever delivered wood to her before?"

"Not to her, sir. It was always Mr. Montague who ordered any stuff before."

"Was he in the habit of ordering wood?"

"Well, he'd had two or three lots when he wanted to build something. He'd got some cattle on the marshes and he had built one or two shelters."

"Those were larger lots?"

"Yes."

"He had never given you such a small order cut to an exact length?"

"No, he always sawed it up himself."

"When Mrs. Montague rang you, was she in a hurry for this wood?"

"Yes, she had to have it that day."

"That was on the Thursday, the day before Mr. Montague was found drowned?"

"Yes."

"You delivered this?"

"Yes, I ran round with it in the van in the afternoon."

"Did you see Mrs. Montague, or Mr. Montague?"

"I saw Mrs. Montague. She told me to leave it round by the landing stage."

"This was unusual?"

"Yes."

"What did she say?"

"She said, 'Just lay it round there for now.' "

The next witness was—

"Girls! What are you all doing here!"

It was Miss Knight. My heart gave a great bound and a flush rose up from my toes.

"What are you all doing clustered round these bushes?"

I crushed the paper and threw it in a ball behind me, my heart pounding.

"It was a bird, Miss Knight." Iris's voice was sure and shrill. "A funny sort of bird with white stripes."

"Yes, it was, it was ever so funny," a chorus said.

"I've never seen anything like it before, Miss Knight. It went into these bushes."

"Well, it's gone now, evidently. Disperse and run about. That's what you are in the fresh air for."

"Yes, Miss Knight," the chorus answered.

"I thought if we could catch it"—Iris was confidential—"Miss Fletcher would be interested—for natural history. I believe I saw it again just now—"

"Well, you keep on looking and the others run about. A thrush, I should say—I don't think we've any penguins here!"

Dutiful laughter rang out.

"Thank you, Miss Knight. I will, Miss Knight."

There was a scampering away, then quietness.

I smoothed the paper out. There were several more witnesses, people I did not know, and then there was me—all I had said printed in the paper! Me! In the papers! The sheet was too crumpled to read it all. I turned it over:

"You are Mrs. Kerrison of Little Snelling, postmistress."

"Yes, sir, and it's a shop as well."

"You knew Mr. Montague?"

"Yes, sir, I didn't see him often, but a nice gentleman."

"How often did you see him?"

"Well, once or twice a week he came to use the phone or post a letter."

"The telephone box is near your gate and the posting box is outside, so you would not see him to speak to."

"No—well, sometimes he came in for stamps or something, but not very often."

"So you couldn't say that you knew him well."

The witness flushed and appeared to take umbrage.

"Well, I should think I knew him as well as most. No one did know 'im. He kept hisself to hisself. He hadn't no one. Why do you think I was called to identify the body! A nice job! He hadn't no one."

"Keep to the point, Mrs. Kerrison. I ask you straight questions and you give me straight answers."

"Yes, sir."

"Now the gardener, Tom Hambling, old Tom as I believe he is called, you know him well?"

"Oh, him, the old lune. Always poking around at nights. Since Mr. Watkins died, his master, he only comes out at night, like a bat he is, except in his garden. Give me the creeps, he do. Never come when I'm open, but come knockin' on the door at night."

"What does he come for?"

"His sweets, hard-boiled ones. How he eats 'em, I don't know, with no teeth, sucks 'em, I suppose. His pension, and then his groceries—sit there he do, mumblin' while I write it down by the candle and Joe ha'ta leave 'em on the step in the morning."

"What about milk and eggs and bread?"

"Specs Joe to go and get them, he do, and take 'em with the groceries—why I do it, I don't know. Too good-natured, that's my trouble—"

"You called him 'the old lune.' Do you consider him mentally deficient?"

"Loony as they come. Always mumblin' and dodderin'. Can't make head or tail of what he say sometimes. Always was a bit wrong in the head, if you ask me, but he's got worse."

"What about his physical strength? Would you say that he is very feeble?"

"Stronger than he lets on, if you ask me. He don't need t' walk like that. He can stand up straight if he like. It's just habit. He had a bit of bronchitis a winter or two ago, and he laid straight enough in bed then. The district nurse, I'd gone to give a hand, said if he could be straight a-lyin' he could a-standin' up."

"How did he get on with Mr. Montague?"

"I've never heard him say, but Mr. Montague hated the sight of him."

"How would you know that if you seldom talked to Mr. Montague?"

"Mrs. Montague said so. She used to laugh and say, 'Poor old man. Rowland hates him so. It must make him feel uncomfortable and unwanted.' "

"But Mr. Montague sent him fruit and a letter, did he not?"

"The first time he's ever sent him anything. Still I s'pose there has to be a first time. A lot of us alter as we get older."

"We have the letter—the letter of which I spoke, m'lord."

"Yes, carry on, Mr. Cameron, but keep your witness to the point. We shall be here all night."

"Yes, m'lord. Old Tom brought you this letter to read for him?"

"Yes, he can't read. Can't write either; he has to make a cross. It makes me feel right bad now, readin' that letter and all the while the poor gentleman were dead lyin' in the water."

"Did he come at night?"

"Yes, it was dark, but he won't come in, pointed to his boots, they were muddy, so I took it under the light an' read it out as he stood by the door."

"What did the letter say?"

"It said, 'I am sorry that I have been unfriendly in the past. One realizes, as one gets older, what loneliness is. Youth betrays one's trust. I feel the need for occasional company of my own age. Would you care to join me in the evenings on the landing stage for a quiet hour's fishing? I shall stroll down that way each evening next week at about eight o'clock.' "

"How did Tom take this?"

"He was pleased. He was all excited like a child. He said, 'He sent me a chicken and some fruit.' "

"And he said that he would go?"

"Yes, he went. He went every night. And then he came to me one night all of a trouble, poor old boy. He'd never seen anyone all the time. So I went and had a look. And Mrs. Montague came out of the house all haughty-like and said, 'What do you want?' She looked different. All pale, as though she had been crying. She said Mr. Montague had gone away."

"But you didn't believe her."

"Well, it seemed funny when he'd asked Tom to meet him."

"So you went to the police."

"Well, I said to Joe, there's something funny goin' on. If there's nothin' in it, there's no harm done, an' when the police came they noticed the sawdust an' the landing stage had been tampered with an' they pulled a board up an' found his body in the muddy water. He'd bin hit on the head, an' the planks had been driven in upright t' stop him floatin' into the river an'—"

"Yes, Mrs. Kerrison. We know the details. Thank you. That will do."

"I thought you'd just like t' know."

The court adjourned.

I looked up, my neck stiff. It was nearly dark in the hut. Although my eyes had gone closer to the page, I hadn't noticed it. There was no sound. They had left me. Panic rose like a shiver of gooseflesh. Oh, God, don't let them have gone into supper. At this moment Miss Knight's sharp eyes were looking round.

"Where"—she would pause with deadly purpose—"is Ann Fielding?"

Oh, God, don't let them have . . . The papers slipped off my lap and scattered. I picked them up hurriedly and laid them in a heap. I unbolted the door, lifted the latch and pushed. Someone had put the chain on the staple and hung the padlock, open, through it on the other side. I pushed again, but it stuck. Tears pricked and flooded my eyes. I pushed again and rattled the door. Then I stood still and looked at it. The door opened to the space of a tiny crack, the chain across the line of grey light. The floor was covered with twigs blown in from under the draughty eaves. I found the thinnest, the strongest, inserted it under the chain and pushed upwards. The outward pressure on the door tightened and the twig broke. The only thing was something long and thin to tip the open ring of the padlock upwards. I folded a paper lengthways and pressed it tightly. I eased it through the crack. I could not see the padlock, but felt, pulling the door as much as possible towards me. There was a tinkle and the door opened. I rushed out, threw the paper in, felt in my pocket for the key. In the deep gloom inside, as I turned, the papers lay on the seat. On the top page was a picture of Miranda. Her hair was cut short as I had last seen it and she lay staring upwards. I shut and locked the door. I would look at it tomorrow. I rushed across the damp grass. A car stood in the drive near the front entrance. I crept around the wall and looked in at the lighted windows. The dining room was empty. Used plates stood on the table. They had had supper. The girls were crowded into the library, some writing, others lolling about. Oh, God, let the side door be still open . . . Oh, God. It gave gently and I slipped into the lighted passage. Just a short run to the library and I was there . . .

"Coo—you're lucky. You would have copped it."

"What did Miss Knight say?"

"She wasn't there. She had supper in her room—with a man," breathed Iris, her face to mine. "Miss Fletcher took supper and we moved up so your place wasn't seen."

"Thank you, Iris. Oh, thank you, Iris."

"I've got the photos here. My mother says will you sign them because she wants to be sending them." She opened her exercise book and brought out a photograph of me cut from the school group and the large one of Miranda from the paper, still with her bouncing curls, pasted on cardboard.

"She says will you put on that one, 'My cousin Miranda, to Iris from her best friend, Ann Fielding,' and on this one, 'To Iris from Ann.' "

The next day was cold and wet. We were kept working hard at our lessons and in the evening, with the wind and rain lashing the windows, were sent to the library.

"No recreation today. A good time to catch up with your prep."

I could not concentrate on the books before me. I wanted to get back to the papers. I lay, when the others were at last asleep, and saw her face, with the short hair, staring upwards—locked in the dark box.

On the next evening the grounds were flooded with golden sunlight. Around the beech tree purple and yellow crocuses had pushed upwards through the damp turf. The girls' interest was fading and I slipped alone to the little hut among the trees. I seized the top paper and began reading.

* * *

On this fifth day of the trial the accused was cross-examined by Mr. Cameron, KC, counsel for the Crown. She stood composed, looking paler and thinner, perhaps, than on the first day, and later, when she had been examined by her own counsel, Mr. Cameron approached to question her again.

"You are Miranda Montague of the Mill House, Little Snelling."

"Yes."

"When you married, you were twenty years of age and your husband was sixty."

"Yes."

"Were you happy?"

"I was very fond of him."

"But you had a lover."

"No, I had a friend."

"You were not lovers?"

"No."

"And yet you intended to go away with him."

"I was in love with him."

"You were in love with him but you were not lovers."

"Yes."

"Had you committed adultery?" Mr. Cameron's voice was soft, the words spoken in his inimitable casual way. The accused did not answer. She stood staring, then tears filled her big dark eyes and flowed silently down her cheeks.

"Had you?"

The words came out like a sudden clap of thunder. Her

wide eyes were fixed on him as though mesmerized.

"Had you?"

"Only once—"

"And when was this?"

"Two nights before—"

"Not on the night before your husband was murdered, but on the night before that?"

"Two nights before he went away."

"Who went away?"

"My husband."

"Your husband was murdered, drowned, he did not go away."

"He said he was going away."

"I put it to you that you murdered your husband. That your lover was going back to Australia. That you knew this and you had to hold him. He needed money. He could have had his farm or anything else if you were left a rich widow. So you were desperate. But two things you did not know. You did not know when you committed this crime that your lover was already on his way. He had left early on the morning of the crime without telling you of the exact day of his going on the night before. Secondly that your husband had changed his will during the week before he died. He had left everything he possessed to Tom Hambling, the gardener."

"It's impossible! He hated him!"

"But he did. People change. Do you not think it was because he knew of your alliance that he did so?"

"No, he would not do that."

"But we have the will, witnessed, signed by his own hand."

"There has been some mistake. He would not leave anything to that man."

"Did you intend to go away with Jeff Mitchell?"

She hung her head and her lips trembled.

"Yes."

"You had told your husband?"

"Yes."

"When did you tell him?"

"On the night before—"

"Was your husband angry?"

"No, he was quite reasonable. We talked it over, and he said that I would be happier with 'this other man,' he called him, and that he had already made arrangements to go away himself."

"Did he say where he was going?"

"Yes, to Canada, he said he had a brother there."

"To Canada—one to Australia and one to Canada. Your men seemed to be leaving in all directions."

"I don't think that remark is quite in order, Mr. Cameron. We are not here to mock."

"I'm sorry, my lord."

"Proceed, Mr. Cameron."

"It would need a lot of arranging to go to Canada. One does not go off just like that. There would be passports, tickets—"

"He said that he had arranged everything. That I could sell the house if I wished. A taxi was arriving for him at eleven o'clock. That is why he sent Ann to old Tom's, to get her out of the way."

"And you sent her for salt that you did not need."

"Yes. I did not want her to come home until after he had gone."

She had lied to me. Miranda had lied to me.

"Did you see him off?"

"No. He asked me especially to keep out of the way. He said he did not wish to cause me pain. He said, 'Go for a walk by the river, by the landing stage. I left an awl lying there. Put it in the shed, and then when Ann comes, you can think of something to say.' "

"You did all this and when the girl, Ann, came, you saw her off in her taxi."

"Yes."

"Why did you order two lengths of wood from Mr. Hatcher?"

"My husband asked me to phone."

"He told you the exact lengths to order?"

"Yes."

"Had he ever asked you to order wood before?"

"No."

"Didn't you wonder at such a small quantity and cut to exact size?"

"He said he was building a shelter."

"With two small pieces of wood?"

"I did not think much about it."

"Why did you tell the man, when he brought it, to put it by the landing stage?"

"My husband had said, 'Tell him to just dump it there. I can easily carry it to where I want it.' "

"I put it to you that you ordered this wood for yourself, that you murdered your husband and required this wood for your purpose."

"No, I did not."

"That you knew that you would have to act quickly, that you had prepared this wood prematurely, using the awl for the holes. That directly your husband settled himself to fish, you struck him with the awl just hard enough to stun him, that he toppled into the water, that you guided his body to under the landing stage with one of the pieces of wood. That you had loosened a plank ready. That you lifted this plank and drove your piles in on the river side of the body to keep it secure. That you then nailed this plank down with the old nails into the top of the new wood in the holes that you had prepared."

"No, I did not."

"That you sent the girl, Ann, to the village shop, knowing full well that she would have to wait, to give you more time for your actions."

"No, that is all untrue."

"Your husband was murdered. He did not go to Canada. He had made no arrangements to go to Canada. He had no passport, no ticket, no taxi came. He had no brother in Canada. He had no relatives at all. How did his body get into the water? The witness, Ann Fielding, saw Tom Hambling at the cottage, so he could not have done it. You were at the landing stage, so it could only have been you."

"I did not do it. I am telling the truth."

The sunlight had gone. There was a rustle of leaves at the back of the hut and something was scratching. It was not so dark as it had been on the other night when I was locked in, but the panicky need for haste seized me. I grabbed one of the other papers and looked at the date. It was the latest one that Iris had brought.

> CHARGE TO THE JURY
>
> Lord Justice Harold: "Members of the jury, you have listened for seven days with great attention to this case. The charge against the prisoner is that of wilful murder. We have here the ancient story of an old man married to a young wife. She takes a lover and—"

There were pages of it, sheets of close print. I could not wait; it would be suppertime and I might not be so lucky again. I bundled the papers together and laid them in a corner. I went out and locked the door. I raced across the grass. I was in time. They were just pouring, chattering and laughing, down the corridor into the dining room. I joined the throng.

The new teacher, long expected, Miss Rose Hancer, had arrived. The girls crowded round her in the library after supper. She had fair hair and cheeks pink like her name.

When she smiled, two dimples receded into deep little holes. Iris and Suzy Parker were vying with each other to make her laugh. The others watched, fascinated. I wanted to tell Jennifer Jackson that I had finished with the papers and she could have the padlock back, but I could not get near. I felt in my pocket. I had lost the key. Oh, well—it didn't matter.

One Thursday night, in the dormitory, all the girls were asleep. Even Iris was exhausted. It was as though we had been thrown up and held on high glittering peaks and now had sunk back onto the soft pillow of normality. Their breathing was a faint rhythm save for the nasal whine of Sally Hodgekiss who had asthma. I was reading in the golden cavern under the bedclothes. I was reading for the hundredth—the thousandth—time of the meeting of Elizabeth Bennet and Darcy at the Hall. Suddenly the door clicked—my light was out, my eyes thin slits. It was Miss Knight and Miss Fletcher. Miss Knight had a torch, the glass tied over with muslin. The soft beam went in an arc around the beds.

"All asleep, thank goodness. The best hour of the day. One can relax."

They stopped by me. My eyes were tightly shut. She bent over my bed. Her breath smelt of smoke and the wine we used to have at Mr. Montague's.

"Fast asleep."

"I wonder if she's dreaming."

"Now you're being sentimental. I assure you things, even like that, pass over these brats."

“Still—quite an experience.”

“Yes. I thought she did quite well.”

“It was her evidence that did it.”

“And a good thing too. Those sort of women think they can get away with anything. Yes, as you say, it was the child’s evidence that hanged her.”

Chapter 9

The excitement of leaving school faded. I was seventeen. The farm was small, isolated. There was a long, straight, treeless drive. My father, a quiet man, bowed with daily work, had withdrawn into a world of his own, whether empty or filled with resources, I did not know. My mother had become more tight-lipped, silent. She never went out, not even to chapel any more. It was as though the trial, the disgrace, had put a final lid on her bitterness. I tried to help, to feed chickens, to gather and chop nettles for the baby turkeys, to clean the house.

"Leave it alone. I'll do it." Her eyes were tired. "Get on with your practising. There is no need for you to roughen your hands with these jobs."

She never forgot that her father had been a chapel parson and the mistake that she had made in marrying my father. She was determined that I should be a lady. Every day I was sent to the icy damp sitting room, to the black piano, to the scales, the arpeggios, the painful exercises, where only the walls listened. Miranda, the trial, the whole business, was never mentioned. A heavy guilt hung over us, pressed us down. I felt marked for life.

And then, one day, my father came into the sitting room where I was gazing from the window watching the March wind bending the poplars.

"I've got something for you in the shed."

It was a bicycle. A bright blue bicycle.

"I picked it up at a sale and I've given it a touch of paint."

For the first time in years I threw my arms round his neck. A tear glistened in the aging eyes beneath the grey brows.

"Get out and about, lass, among your friends and stop brooding. You don't like music, do you?"

"No." I laughed. It was such a relief to say it.

"No, well, don't tell your mother. She's set her heart on it. She's never forgotten how she used to play pieces at gatherings at the manse. Just give it a rest."

A new world opened. I skimmed to the village. I went to see Iris Baltrop. Whereas Mother never mentioned the trial, Mrs. Baltrop talked of nothing else. It gradually came over me that I was regarded as a celebrity. I was asked to tea and one or two friends dropped in to look at me, to talk to me. It was exciting and yet uncomfortable, as though I was an interesting piece of china or a new film at the Regal.

The Baltrops lived above and behind the shop. They

had had a wing built on at the back and the house "done over."

"And about time too," said Mrs. Baltrop.

"This," said Iris proudly, "is the lounge."

It took my breath away. Tall lamps, "They're standards," said Iris, had large coloured shades of red, yellow and purple. The carpet was bright blue and great chairs stood about. A line of china geese went up one wall.

"This is for cocktails," said Iris. She lifted the lid and a light came on, glinting rows of bottles. "No pictures," she said. "Pictures are not fashionable. Would you like to see the toilet?"

It was all pink. Fluffy mats and a mirror with pink roses on the glass across the corner. There was a pink bath and a pink washbasin.

"Pink toilet and all," said Iris, lifting the lid.

We went down to tea and there were pink cakes on dishes with doilies—pink seemed to be Mrs. Baltrop's favourite colour—a lace tablecloth, jam in a china pot with a silver lid and spoon, and paper roses in a vase. Mrs. Baltrop's hair was fuzzy and her breath smelt of violets.

"Are you going to the dance at the Hut on Saturday?" whispered Iris as I went to get my coat.

"I don't know. I don't know what I've got on."

I had never been to a dance and I never had anything on, but I was not telling Iris.

"There's been a lot of trouble there." She looked round to see that we were alone. "Couples have been going out! Mrs. Winter and a lot of other old bags complained and set the police to watch. And do you know"—her face was close to mine and the familiar nausea made me turn my head—"one was Sergeant Murray's own daughter!"

The front door was open as I cycled up the drive and my mother stood in the doorway.

"Just leave your bike there and put it away later. Your father's having a bath in the kitchen. Grumbling and grousing, you never heard the like, but I've finally got him into it. I've put the tea in here."

There was a fire in the sitting room. Rabbit pie, chutney, and the big brown teapot stood on the table.

"I've had mine. I had it at Iris Baltrop's."

"You'll have a proper tea here now. Sit up." The kettle on the hob was boiling. Mother measured three spoonfuls from the tea caddy into the teapot and turned to the fire.

"I shouldn't keep going there if I were you. She was his mother's maid. She used to come to the back door to see our maid at the manse. My mother was always hustling her off."

She poured the tea, brown and strong, and the knife was poised over the pie. The crust was golden, shining, with a wavy edge. I watched, fascinated. It was like taking the first step onto smooth untrodden snow. The point struck between a pastry rose and a leaf and cut downwards. A pale leg hung to the white underside of the triangular slice and landed precariously on my waiting plate. The jelly squelched as she lifted the upturned egg cup with a knife. She added a dab of fat pork and a mound of brown chutney by the side.

"There. Be eating that. I'll just see to your father. Making a rare mess, I'll be bound."

The fire was smoking. I ate the pie. It was good. I helped myself to another leg. My mother came back carrying the lighted lamp. It smelt of paraffin.

"He'll be half an hour yet." She took the pot and put it in the hearth. "A good thing it's only once a week."

"I'm going to the dance at the Hut on Saturday night."

"That you're not."

"Yes, I am."

She sat down and began eating. I looked at her. Her iron-grey hair was drawn back into a bun. She had married late in life and had been forty when I was born. Her high tucked dress under her apron had a tiny frill edging and was fastened at the neck with a cameo.

"You can put that out of your mind," she said.

I got up.

"Where are you going?"

"I've finished. I'll just go down the garden before it gets dark and I'll put the bike away."

The WC was behind currant bushes. It was like the old abandoned one at school. It had a box of newspaper in the corner and a tin of disinfectant. There was a square hole in the wall above the door, and in this, things lodged. I sat and watched, the spider's web across the corner, it was thick and grey, the bits of straw, the pile of birds' droppings. I put my hand down to the paper carefully. I was always afraid that a rat would jump out at the tearing sound.

Mother was still sitting there when I went back.

"Sally Winter's going," I said.

My heart beat. My face flushed—the truth and nothing but the truth—my hands sweated. I waited to be struck dead.

"Her mother doesn't mind."

Mother had gone slightly pink. She kept her eyes down at her plate.

"Well—you're seeing her there, are you?"

"Yes, we'll go on our own."

"Well, in that case—you can go if your father takes you. He will drive you in the trap and come and fetch you."

I felt sick as I went to bed. I didn't really want to go. I had told my mother a lie. It shut me off from her—for ever. It was the pink bathroom that had broken my heart.

Chapter 10

My father helped me down from the trap.

"Don't forget now. Out before the music stops and I'll be right here."

"Yes, all right."

"Don't forget now."

He turned the horse round and drove away, the carriage lights dying into the distance. I stood on the gravel. The windows were blue checkered squares. The whine of a violin sounded above the thump of a piano. I opened the door. The floor was empty. It was fawn and dusty. Chairs stood round the edge in silent rows. On the dais at the far end was the band, four people in evening dress. They looked at me as I came in. The woman's long black skirt spread over the piano stool. She had ginger hair and bare arms and tossed her head to the music and called something to the others as I hesitated. I glanced back. Behind was the bare empty gravel, before me the empty floor. I stood, frightened to move.

"Shut the door, dear."

I jumped.

Behind the door, on a small table, were glasses and bottles of lemonade. A fat motherly woman smiled.

"You're letting the cold in, dear."

"I'm sorry."

"You all alone then?"

"I'm meeting a friend here."

"No one'll come for another hour or two yet. It's allus the same. Come when the pubs close."

"I'll just put my coat away."

"It's a shilling, dear, the ticket. I take the money."

"Oh."

I found the coin. I looked at the cool lemonade. My throat was dry, but the shilling was all I had. The band had stopped playing. The men were wiping their mouths, their instruments. They all seemed to have large white handkerchiefs. I looked up the long length of the floor to the door to the left of the dais. A notice was scrawled in chalk, "Ladies." Then I started to walk. I reached it. I shut the door. I was in. I was alone, away from the eyes.

It was small, of stained rough wood. Folding tables were stacked in the corner. A mirror stood on a stool leaning against the wall. There was one chair. Someone had intended to paint it. It had been scrubbed, the wood was grey and bare, with small dabs of blue on back and legs. I tried the paint with a finger. It was dry. I sat down, my heart beating. I got my handkerchief, starched, white, from my pocket and wiped the palms of my hands. The music had started again. I went to the mirror. It was too low. It showed my buckled patent shoes, my fawn stockings, the full skirt of my blue velveteen dress. I lowered myself, knees bent, and there was the tight bodice, the long sleeves, the white lacy collar. My face was pale, my fair hair waving from the curlers that I had kept on all the night before, that had woken me digging into my head. Suddenly I must, I wanted to go to the lavatory, I must —the sharp urgency gripped me. I sat down. It got worse. Panic slowly came in a wave. Sweat broke on my forehead, my hands. What was that door? It had an iron latch. Please, God, don't let it be locked. Don't let it be a kitchen —with somebody there—or anything. I tried it gently. It opened to the night. Just outside, across long damp grass, was a small corrugated tin shelter. I went in. It had no top. There was emptiness. I bopped desperately. I got back into the cloakroom, my heart hammering. The edge of my skirt was soiled, my shoes wet and muddy. I rubbed the velvet with my handkerchief. I rubbed my shoes. They were still not clean. The handkerchief was black, sodden. I opened the door and flung it away. There was no water, nothing. Tears pricked my eyes. I looked all round. Behind the tables was a pile of old Christmas decorations—paper streamers—pink crepe paper. I tore at it and rubbed desperately. I used it dry, I damped it in the grass outside. Soon my shoes were fairly clean. I sat down, my tears dried. My face! I bent to the mirror, rubbing my cheeks with the pink paper. Then I sat down again. The music stopped and there—I listened—was a faint sound of clapping.

I opened the door to a long sliver of the hall. Two girls were leaving the floor. I didn't know them. I shut the door and went back to the chair. What was the time? I had come at half-past seven. Where were the others? It must be late. The band struck up again. The music was quicker, livelier. Suddenly laughter bubbled, calling, and running feet. The door burst open and there was Iris, bright with life. There was Rose Howlet from the pub, fat Suzy Parker, Doris, Peggy, and Jennifer Jackson. Several girls I didn't know stared.

"What are you doing here?" Iris shrieked. "How long have you been here?"

"Oh, I've only just come."

"That's a lie. Old mother Jennings at the door said you came at half-past seven. Don't you know it's no good coming early? Haven't you ever been to a dance before?"

They took off their coats. They all wore lipstick. Heavy earrings hung from Iris's pointed ears. Rose Howlet's black dress had a low back. Their scent filled the little room.

"Haven't you got a dance dress?"

"I didn't have time to change. I've been out."

"Where?"

My face flamed.

"To my aunt's over at Hickling."

"Oh—" Iris's eyes were disbelieving. "I thought perhaps your mother wouldn't let you wear a dance dress."

They all laughed.

"Want a cachou? They're some of my mother's. I pinched 'em."

She handed them round to the others—would she . . . ?

"Here you are. Do you want one? Well, are we all ready?"

I got into the middle of the group and we trooped out. Several couples were dancing. We sat by the wall.

"Come on." Iris pulled my hand. "We might as well have a go."

We had danced at school—the polka, the foxtrot, the valeta. Iris put her face close to mine. The violet mingled with her breath.

"You been using rouge?"

"A little, why?"

"I don't know—your face looks funny."

"I've got a cold."

"Wait till Rex Armstrong and all that lot come—things'll liven up."

"What time do they get here?"

"When the pubs close." She looked at me incredulously. "I'm going out if he asks me. He took Jane Barton out last time, but she isn't here tonight."

I danced with Rose, Suzy, Peggy, Jennifer. There were only two men in the room and they had partners. And then, suddenly, there was a stamping, a rattle, and the door was flung open. Men poured in. They were red-faced, shouting. One or two younger boys at the back were paler, swaying sheepishly.

"Come on, boys, pay up."

"But it's nearly over."

"You pay up, or out you go."

"Well, come on, let's go. It don't look worth much."

They turned in a body.

"Half price, then."

"What do you think, Rex? Half price?"

"Aw, come on, get it over with."

The music stopped. We sat in a row. My heart was hammering.

"That's Rex Armstrong," whispered Iris.

He was taller, older than the others. He was broad and red-faced. He had long narrow hands.

"His people have got a farm up the road. Quite near yours. They haven't been there long. Haven't you ever heard of them?"

"No."

Since the trial I never heard of anyone.

The music started. One of the band suddenly got up and said, "Take your partners for the foxtrot."

I suppose he thought it hadn't been worth it before. One of the boys lurched across and asked Iris to dance. Then one of the pale-faced youths at the back was pushed forward and came nervously towards me. He bent and took Suzy Parker's hand. I sat with an empty chair on either side. I coughed and bent to tighten the buckle on my shoe.

I felt for my handkerchief and remembered I hadn't one. The woman behind the lemonade watched me. The dance finished. Their partners took Iris and Suzy for lemonade. I still sat on.

"Take your partners for the waltz."

My face ached with smiling. The boys at the door were looking at me and laughing and saying something to Rex Armstrong. He started to walk towards me. He was grinning and swaying slightly. He was coming towards me—there was no one else. He stopped and nearly fell over. He wore brown shoes.

"Dance?"

I got up. My knees were stiff. His tie was dark red. He hummed as we danced. I glanced up, but he was looking above my head across the room.

"Does your mother know you're out?"

"She knows I'm here."

He laughed.

"You still at school?"

"No, I'm seventeen."

Several boys in the corner started to whistle and he grinned at them.

The dance finished. I stood still. Would he take me to a seat, would he? He turned and walked off. I went to the ladies. I sat on the chair. The next dance started. I still sat there. Then I got up and went into the hall and sat down just inside in the corner by the dais of the band. He was dancing with Iris Baltrop. She was looking up into his face and he was looking down and smiling. It was a secret smile. It was as though he was not listening to what she was saying but smiling at something he was thinking. The dance ended, she hung on his arm. She walked with him to the lemonade table. She brought out her purse from her silver bag and paid for two glasses. He drank facing the room, staring across her head. She still looked up, talking and gesticulating. I did not see him speak once.

"Take your partners for the last dance."

He put his glass down and came straight towards me.

"Dance?"

The doorway was empty. The boys were dancing; now or never. We went once round the room, then he steered me towards it.

"Comin' out for a breath of fresh air?"

The night was cold—starry. He put his arm round me, walking across the gravel. He steered me to the dark corner by the side of the Hut. His arms were tight around me, lifting me off my feet, pressing me against the wall. His teeth hurt my lips. One hand was on my thigh . . .

"No."

I wrenched away.

"Aw, come on."

I went back. He had brought me out—instead of Iris Baltrop. All the whisperings, the tales, the jokes that I had heard at school were wrong. I was filled with curiosity, excitement.

His hand moved to my body. I broke away laughing and ran to the door. The dance had just ended. Everybody looked up as I went across to get my coat. The girls in the cloakroom stopped jabbering and stared.

"Well, you're a nice one!"

"You're a dark horse!"

Iris Baltrop went out. She tossed her head and did not speak. I bent and looked in the mirror. My eyes were shining. My cheeks were pink.

He was waiting in the doorway.

"I'll see you home."

"I'm going with my father."

He put up his head, calling to the boys behind him.

"She's goin' with her father!"

They all laughed. He looked down at me with that secret look.

"See you along the road sometime."

I went hot. Waves of excitement washed over me. My father was waiting.

"You're late, lass. I said just before the end."

He bent over, putting the rug round my legs as I climbed in.

"I'm sorry, Father."

"Well, never mind, if you enjoyed it."

Chapter 11

I went out with Rex for two years. I was Rex's girl. My life was supposed to be filled with visits to Sally Winter—tennis parties—helping with "At homes." I saw her once in the draper's shop at Bincome. She was with her mother. They were beautifully dressed. Mrs. Winter held the lead of a small Pekingese in her gloved hand. She nodded slightly and Sally said "Hello." I looked at her, this mythical companion of my mother's dreams.

I lay at night in bed, while the wind howled, dreaming of Rex. And in the heat of the summer I was filled with delicious memories—of his hands, his voice, his shivering secret look. He had an old car, a Ford with a big black hood, and we went far afield. We went to pubs where I sat in the corner while he leaned on the counter talking and laughing to the barmaid or his friends. I watched the broad back—he is mine, mine, and I quivered, waiting for the ride home.

On one hot summer afternoon I rode on my bicycle along the hedgerows. I was out of the way of my mother's look, her voice. I rode slowly. If I kept going—a long, long way—it would fill in the time until I met Rex. All time was to be filled in till I met Rex. I went through a village and came to a long straight road. It seemed familiar, and then, just ahead, under the great tree, was the village shop by the Mill House. I stopped, one foot on the bank. To my left, level with the handlebars, was the gap where I had pushed through. It had become slightly grown over. A sudden feeling of excitement and curiosity gripped me. I laid the bike on the bank. The twigs scratched my legs. I was out in the rough meadow. I walked across the grass. I went towards the trees surrounding Tom's cottage. Was he still there? Was he dead? I walked through the dark bushes and pushed open the little gate. I was in the small hot vegetable garden. Old Tom was bent, putting in plants. His glasses had fallen off onto the ground beside him. Their gold side pieces stuck into the air.

"Good morning, Tom," I said.

He jumped. He almost sprang upright. Then he grabbed the glasses without looking at me and scuttled into the house.

Poor Tom—I laughed to myself at his shock—I hope he didn't hurt his back. It was like a dream. Everything exactly the same, as though a film had unrolled, been folded up, put away, and was now unrolled again. Was the Mill House empty? Were the grounds wild, overgrown, unkept? I went on. Trim grass met my eye, roses in full bloom. The sound of the weir was a dull roar. The familiar remembered scent of box hedges and jasmine drifted, warm, soft—I drew deep breaths. I walked on the gravel round to the front of the house. To the left, at the side, baked in the sun, were the pale brick terraces, the loganberry ripe against the wall, the ramblers hanging pink nodding heads. I looked up at the windows, the white canopied door. They were clean, there were curtains, someone was living there.

I would go round by the river. I felt brave, adventurous. If I met anyone, I was a lady novelist looking for material; I had heard the place was for sale and was looking round; I had come back from abroad and this was the home of my ancestors.

I turned the corner by the house. A man stood in front of me. He was rather short and fat. He wore fawn-stained trousers, a white shirt open at the neck. A cap was pulled down on curly iron-grey hair. His brown eyes looked from under the shadow of the peak, the corners crinkling into a smile. He carried a basket.

"Why, it's the little girl at the trial."

A tension of the forehead, a holding of breath, relaxed, melted—the little girl at the trial. It was so ordinary—like the little girl at the tennis match.

"Were you there?"

"No, I saw your photograph in the paper."

That awful old photograph—I smoothed my blue gingham.

"I hope I don't look anything like that now."

"Oh, much prettier." He was still, watching me, his eyes warm with the smile.

"I was just passing and I thought I would like to look round again. I didn't know if anyone lived here. I'm sorry."

"Oh, don't be. It was perfectly natural."

He held out his hand.

"Bernard Hales."

Bernard—it fitted him. He was round and pleasant. It was funny, I thought, how names did fit people—Mr. Montague, sharp, pointed—Tom—Rex—I looked across to where the river crashed over the weir into the pool.

Miranda . . .

"You know mine," I said.

"Yes—well"—he turned briskly—"would you like to come into the house, or look round the garden first?"

The house; of course, all the old furniture would be gone, all the old owls cleared out, the photographs—perhaps he had furniture like Iris Baltrop's, red carpets, a cocktail cabinet, standard lamps.

"Have you electricity?"

"Yes, I have my own generator. It runs off batteries."

"I would like to see inside the house."

"Well, come along. You should, you know. It's like recovering from a bad accident. One should go straight back. It chases away the bogeys."

We went together up the front steps and he opened the door and stood aside.

I felt flat disappointment. The grey marble floor with its

tiny diamonds of black was still there. A long faded rug lay on its cold surface. An old oak chest, not better, even older than the one we had at home, stood by the wall. And pictures, dark gloomy pictures, Iris had said pictures were not fashionable, in dim gilt frames, covered the walls and went up by the side of the bare stone staircase.

"Oh, you haven't altered it much."

He had taken off his hat. His head and face were very brown. The top of his head was bald, with the iron-grey hair, thick and rather fluffy, around. He smiled, the wrinkles a little star deepening his eyes.

"No, you think I should?"

"Well, I suppose it could be brightened up—" Embarrassment, politeness, flushed my face. "It's very nice."

"Ah—the drawing room—the sitting room—whichever you prefer—"

It looked huge and bare. The sunshine from the French doors lay like a golden chute on the pale worn carpet. It was of faint pinks and greens and mauves. I looked away from the light. Near my feet was a frayed hole and a large darn. On the walls were long panels of—it looked like needlework. They were of the same pale colours as the carpet and there were shepherdesses and flowers and leaves and little fauns with collars. Between the panels were light brackets with tiny cream shades. The furniture, the cabinets, the chairs with curved legs, were creamy, they looked dirty to me, and were covered with tiny cracks. The pale blue damask chairs by the window were frayed and, in places, faded.

"You like my Aubussons?"

Aubussons—what were they?

"They're very nice," I said.

It wasn't a bit like Iris Baltrop's. We went into the hall.

"Ah, the study. I expect you'd like to see in there again. I'll just put the kettle on while you browse around."

The study was to the east away from the afternoon sun. My heart gave a jump as I went in. The old brown paper was still on the walls but the oars were gone, the stuffed fish and the school groups were gone. Instead there were more pictures, and, on one wall, a huge map stuck with flags. The familiar book shelves were full of books, there were brown leather chairs, and a desk, larger than Mr. Montague's, stood by the window. It was quiet. There was a hush as though something waited, listening.

The door was ajar. It was again that morning. If I turned my head, Miranda was standing there. Mr. Montague was bending slightly, sealing the envelope. I was looking at the walls. They were barer, several of the books were missing—the desk was tidier—I could see the green leather top with the tiny gold edging that I had never seen before—the papers were gone . . .

There was a clatter of cups, a call.

"The tea, such as it is, is on the table."

How silly of me. It was Mr. Hales' study, with a big brown desk with no leather top. They hadn't asked me—if the books and papers had made any difference, they would have asked me.

The door of the kitchen stood open, the warm sunshine

coming up the pinky steps. The dresser was still there and the same old big deal table. Mr. Hales' eyes smiled, watching my face.

"They were thrown in when I acquired the house."

The house—it had been left all alone.

There was no cloth. A big brown teapot like my mother's stood on the bare yellow of the table. A large spoon stood upright in the jar of jam. There was a plate of buns with shiny brown tops and butter in a china dish. The teacups in the sunshine were nearly transparent, their roses suspended in a milky haze.

He laughed and spread his hands.

"A poor spread. Buns from the village baker's. All an old bachelor is capable of." The hot tea tumbled into the cups, the brown level getting higher and higher. I waited for them to crack.

"Do you live here by yourself?"

"Yes, I do. All my life I've dreamed of being alone. People, people, people, all one's life. At school, work, all the time—" He smiled. "I'm referring to mobs of people, you understand."

"Do you look after yourself then? The cooking? The housework?"

"Oh, I'm a dab hand with the frying pan, the odd chicken, the casserole, and then, of course"—he laughed—"there is always Bob Powley's, the baker's, and Mrs. Kerrison's tinned salmon."

I dropped an island of red jam onto the yellow butter on my bun. I held the large spoon, embarrassed.

"Pop it back into the jar."

The last of the old strain dropped from me. I felt it going, draining away. He was warm, comfortable.

"And then I am always busy," he said.

"What do you do?"

"Ah, now, that's a secret, a great secret."

"Oh, do tell me."

I leaned forward smiling and his brown eyes looked straight into mine. They had tiny hazel lines radiating from the black pupil. The lashes were thick and black. The brows were bushy, iron-grey.

"Oh, do tell me," I said.

"Perhaps one day—you must come again."

"Oh, I should love to."

"Let's see now, what do I remember, you live at Kiln Farm, Bampton, and you're at school at Walton."

"Oh, I left ages ago."

He poured more tea.

"And what do you do now?"

"Nothing really." What did I do? I waited for Rex, I got through the day waiting for Rex.

"You help your mother?"

"She won't let me. She wants me—to be a lady." I laughed, then blushed hotly, it sounded so silly.

"To be a lady is to do nothing, a common misapprehension. I expect you get bored."

"Oh, I do."

He sat looking at me. One hand and arm rested on the table. The hand was scrubbed clean with faint grey lines around the nails. When he had stood outside holding the basket, it had been covered with clay.

"Would you care to come along and help me?"

I stared, my cheeks flushing. To come to the Mill House, to be at the Mill House all day! To be busy so that the hours fled speeding to the long warm evening with Rex . . .

"Oh, I would, I would love it. I could cook and scrub—"

"Not so fast." He laughed, his eyes went tiny in the star of wrinkles. "I will do the scrubbing. No, I was thinking that you could help me with something else. How far is it to Bampton?"

"Oh, about five or six miles. I have a bike."

"I think it would be best"—he was suddenly serious—"if your mother came to see me. Would she do that? I could explain to her"—he gave a slight smile—"that it's all perfectly respectable."

My mother went. It was the first time that she had been out or spoken to anyone other than ourselves since the trial. The taxi brought her back after tea. I was fretting to be gone to where the car waited by Foxes Copse around the corner. She stood aggravatingly slowly taking the pins from her hat. I had a dim memory, a thin wraith, of her standing just so before.

"A very nice gentleman," she said, "and clever too. He is doing important work. It will be a very good post for you."

Chapter 12

I stood in the kitchen. It was exciting. There had been a note propped against the teapot.

"Back in an hour or two. Make yourself some coffee."

I was all alone. I knew what he meant when he said that he liked to be alone. I was myself. I gave a little skip. I could explore all on my own. I hadn't been to the next floor. The bathroom! Perhaps it was all pink like Iris Baltrop's! I raced up the stone stairs sometimes taking two at a time, then stopping on alternate ones giving a little hop. I stood outside the heavy door, one, two, three—I opened it with a flourish. It was just the same. It hadn't even any curtains. The white bath with the sprigs of blue flowers surrounded by the great mahogany seat, the lavatory like a big chair in the corner, the washbasin with its blue posies and heavy brass plug and chain, even the small fretwork of cracks and the faint brown stain around the hole—it was all the same—the only difference was an old blue and grey rug on the oak floor, something like the one that I had seen in the hall. Sick disappointment flattened me, emptied me, then joy rose gushing. One day, soon, I would marry, marry—my body warmed, my cheeks bent smiling with uncontrollable thoughts—I would marry Rex: I said the word to capture it, realize it, face its blinding rapture. And we would have a lounge like Iris Baltrop's and a pink bathroom and—

I stood on the landing. There was the door of the room with the great wardrobes full of old clothes that Miranda and I . . . I turned the handle. It was locked.

"Are you there?"

I jumped. I looked down. He stood in the hall looking up. He had the basket in his hand and his shoes were covered with dirt.

"Oh! the mess."

"Now then"—he turned, laughing—"we have no nagging in this house. A little dust here and there—"

I followed him into the kitchen. The basket was on the table between us. It was covered with a grey cloth. He saw me watching, waited till I was seated, then whipped the covering off.

"Ah! The moment of revelation!"

The basket was full of bits of grey stone.

"You are disappointed?" He laughed. "You expected a rabbit—or something?"

"Well, I don't really know—"

"To the uninitiated these are just bits of stone, but to the archaeologist—" He kissed his fingers in rather a silly gesture. "There you have my secret."

Archaeologist? What was that? Archangel? Perhaps it was something to do with religion.

"I have a mound, a burial mound all to myself. Had you noticed it when you stayed here?"

"No."

"Someone had made shallow steps and planted nasturtiums on top."

"Oh, you mean the old hill at the back of the shrubbery."

"The very place. I saw it first some years ago. While on a return visit to Cambridge. I flew over—flying was a sport in those days—and there it was beneath me. I suppose I'm a selfish secretive sort of blighter. I never mentioned it to a soul, although I was a member of a keen archaeological society, and they were hunting for sites. When the war was over, I went with an expedition to Egypt, digging. But I never liked digs with crowds of people. There is not the same feeling; one cannot savour the fullness of one's finds. One should sit mesmerized over the small piece of stone and let the mind travel backwards over centuries."

I was hungry. I hadn't made myself coffee as he said. He sat there with a little triangular chip in his open hand talking slowly as though to himself.

"After digs in Greece I came back to England—about eight years ago—and flew again over this place. I didn't dare think that it would still be the same, but the mound hadn't been touched."

"But how did you get the house? Oh, I suppose it belonged to Tom. You bought it from him."

"Through his solicitors. I have never seen the old boy. When I first saw the mound all those years ago, I made enquiries and it then belonged to a Mr. Watkins. When I came back from abroad, I was told by the local estate agents that it belonged to a Mr. Montague and I left my name with them with a dim hope."

"Oh, you did not know Mr. Montague. You have never seen him."

"No. So you can imagine that I took quite an interest in the case when it was in all the papers. I was in Worcestershire at the time. And so it came about that you were no stranger to me."

"Yes, I see."

"But you're hungry. You've had no coffee? No empty cup? We will eat and then I will show you around."

He brought chops from the stone-shelved larder.

"I will do that."

"I will grill. I have had years of doing for myself in various tents dotted about the world. I assure you that it's no hardship. You can slice potatoes, but don't tell your mother. You are my archaeological assistant!"

It was pleasant eating there. We had fresh peaches and wine that seemed familiar.

"It came with the house. It was in the cellars. Rather

dishonest of me perhaps, but I paid a good price—" He spread his hands and laughed.

I felt warm, excited.

"Now I will show you my treasures."

We went up the stairs to the locked door. He turned the handle.

"It's locked," I said. The smile died from his face and he frowned.

"Ah yes, you were trying it when I came in."

I flushed.

"I'm sorry. I thought you wouldn't mind. It used to be full of old clothes and—" I looked up at him and the frown cleared like a passing shadow. The teasing smile came back.

"And when you found it locked, you thought that there was some mystery, that I was a Bluebeard, perhaps—" He took the key from his pocket and the door opened with a slight creak.

All the wardrobes, the bed, the dressing table with the photographs, the carpets, the curtains, were gone. The sun had left the southeast and it was dull and gloomy. Dust was everywhere, and, in corners, and spread like paths, were piles of stones. A half skull grinned by one window, and great bones were propped behind the door.

"Interesting, those"—he stroked one with a finger—"some large mammal—"

On the wall on the right-hand side was a huge mirror. The room behind stretched into the distance. By the sides of the dull gilt frame of the mirror and round the walls were two tiers of shelves sloping like the lectern that we had had in the school chapel. They were of rough yellow wood and a saw, sawdust, and a bag of nails lay underneath.

"What do you think of my handiwork?" He spread his hand around.

"They are very nice."

He laughed.

"Well, I don't know about nice. They are utilitarian. It is in here that I want you to get busy. We must have several lessons first, of course. And then, when you know what each piece is, they can all be docketed and catalogued. The idea is to display on the shelves."

I had been, with the school, on a visit to a museum. I had seen the tiny hummingbirds, the gorillas, the antelope, the tigers snarling from their dried grass lair. I hadn't taken much notice of the old grey stones, but I remembered them now, with little white tickets, on shelves like these. And the optician's—the smart optician's—with the spectacle frames on red velvet.

"Couldn't we cover the shelves with red velvet and have little white tickets?"

He bent his head to one side, seriously considering.

"I don't think red would be quite suitable, but black—yes, black velvet would be a good idea, stop them from slipping."

"And white cards?"

"And white cards. I can see you are quite a showman!"

"And couldn't we call the room something? Give it a

name? The Crypt! All creepy with those old bones and things—"

He laughed, his head thrown back.

"Is that how you feel about it? Let me see. Crypt—underground vault—burying place beneath a church—if I remember my dictionary correctly. Now this is higher—" he spread his hands, his eyes glinting merriment—"lower, higher—I suppose, as it's just between you and me. We could forget this little point of distinction and elevate from the lower to the above from the beneath—"

"Yes, and we could call it the Upper Crypt, couldn't we?"

I left after tea. I did not go home. I cycled about the lanes until it was time to meet Rex. Then I put my bicycle in Foxes Copse and waited. I sat on the dry needled ground under a pine tree and played with the old cones. I tossed one as a marker and then threw the others to hit it—"*He'll* be here in a minute—one minute—two minutes—if I don't think about it, he'll be here in a minute." I looked at the little silver watch that I had had for my birthday. He was ten minutes late. I got up and turned round and sat again with my back to the road. If I don't look—if I gaze at the trees, if I don't think about it, he'll be here in a minute. He'll be right behind me and I won't have noticed him, one, two, three. I won't say anything to him about being late. I will have forgotten that we were supposed to meet. I was just cycling this way, and I've only just come. I threw the fir cone marker. An hour passed, but when I looked at my watch, it was only twenty minutes. One minute, two minutes, three minutes—if I don't think about it, he'll be here in a minute—one minute, two minutes. My heart gave a bound. The old car came round the corner. I rushed, feet flying. I was in.

"You're late," I said.

He did not speak. He was smiling his secret smile. I snuggled up to him.

"Why are you late, Rex? I've been waiting for ages."

He sat there without looking at me, without moving. I couldn't get through to him. I had never got through to him. There was something that the secret smile hid. His hand was on the wheel. It was long, narrow, red, surprisingly soft and well kept for a worker on the land. I wanted to lift it and put it to my face. If he would touch my cheek, stroke my hair—something, someday, will happen and everything will alter. Always I held back. No, Rex, no, when he held me roughly, touching my body, if he would —stroke my face, touch my hair, kiss my eyelids, talk to me—oh, talk to me, Rex—tell me that he loved me. I dare not say the word—loved me—loved me . . .

"Some of us have got t' work for a living."

"Oh, I am working. I'm working at the Mill House. I started this morning."

"For that old fellar? He's a nut case."

It all bubbled inside me, a burst of talk, about the Mill House, old Tom, the lawns, the flowers, Mr. Hales, what I was doing—but *that* was a secret, a secret, I had a secret from Rex! But it dried up, it didn't come out, he wouldn't understand.

"You want t' mind what you get up to. Alone there all day. Those old boys are the worst."

I looked from the hot stuffy car across the meadow. I felt a lonely shaft, like a little cold finger, a slight detachment from him.

"It isn't a bit like that."

Then something welled up. It warmed my body right from my toes. I looked at him, the rapture breaking my face in an uncontrollable smile. Rex was jealous.

Chapter 13

At the Mill House in October, we picked the apples, the pears. I spread them on straw in the loft above the big coach house while Mr. Hales bumped up the stout ladder at intervals with the laden skeps. The blemished, the bruised, were piled near the opening for immediate use, but the perfect were laid carefully by the far wall. I knelt and made little pockets in the straw for, here a Sopsy Wine, a Doctor Harvey, and then a hard golden-brown flecked pear. They looked pretty, I thought, when I had finished, the red, the ivory, the gold, like the patchwork quilt on my bed at home. My back was aching. I straightened and got up. A faint smell of meal, of corn, lay beneath the heavy scent of the fruit. From the dusty window motes danced in the sunlight, and the shaft of star-spangled gauze reached the apples, the pears, turning them to stained glass. It was quiet. The sound of the weir was muffled, a steady roar, like the drone or hum of bees.

I stood waiting. A slight agitation made me nervous. I listened, a breathless listening, then something touched my cheek: a softness, a caress of down. There was a faint sound—like a sigh—"Look" a silent voice seemed to say —or was it my own thoughts? I walked up the golden shaft to the small high window. I could see right into old Tom's front garden. He was bending over—yes—the rockery. There had been a rockery in the far corner. He looked, in the distance, as though he was demolishing it, pulling the stones away. Suddenly he stood nearly upright, a huge rock in his arms, and hurled it away. Mrs. Kerrison was right—"He's stronger than he lets on—He can stand up straight if he likes—" was he cunning as well? How he must have hated Mr. Montague—knowing that he resented him being there, his old home since he was a boy, his father's before him. When he went to Mrs. Kerrison's that first time after the murder—to tell her of the food and the invitation to fish with Mr. Montague on the landing stage—"he went every night. And then he came to me one night all of a trouble, poor old boy. He'd never seen anyone all the time. So I went and had a look." Had he grown impatient—had he wanted the body to be discovered—had he led her—had he? The sigh touched my face—a faint breath.

"Are you there? Heave ho!"

Mr. Hales's beaming face, like one of the apples, came beheaded through the opening.

In January there was severe frost. The river carved a wavy edge in the bank's white rim and flocks of birds settled on the lawn looking for food. In the attic Mr. Hales found two old pairs of skates. There was a long wide ditch fed by the mill pool and this was frozen thick and solid. He was there one morning when I arrived, skimming the surface. With a cocoon of jacket, thick white socks, turned-over boots, and a wool hat with a large pompon, he looked roly-poly. He waved, red-cheeked, laughing.

"Come and try!"

He knelt, fixing my skates, then held me up. He put his arm round my shoulders, steadying me.

"Careful, slide one foot forward a little and then the other."

I felt wild excitement, a secret sense of mischief. I could skate. My father, who had lived in the Fens in his youth, had taught me to skate all those years ago, before I had gone away to school, when he had been young and bright, before he had become silent and weary. "You never forget, lass," he had said. "It's like riding a bicycle; you never forget."

"Easy now, stand upright, don't bend backwards."

I moved haltingly forward, his hand gripping my arm, then suddenly I broke away. I skimmed swiftly over the long length of ice, sun sparkling on glass between fluffy white banks, turned and came back. I could see him waiting, his arms held forward. I shut my eyes in the fresh wind. It was Rex waiting there—if it was Rex waiting there—waiting as I skimmed towards him, his arms outstretched. It *was* Rex. I raised my lids to the blinding rapture and looked straight into Mr. Hales's eyes. He whitened, his face was suddenly different, thinner, sharper. Then the colour flooded back and he smiled.

"Are you cross?"

"No, it was I who looked foolish." He looked down teasingly. "Women were deceivers ever."

We piled wood into the kitchen stove, fried sausages, and drank wine.

"Where are my specimens?" I said. "What about my work today?"

"Well, I could take a pickaxe, but suppose I ruined something beautiful, golden earrings, or an ancient queen's crown. No, I think today will be a holiday."

The sunlight, the sparkle on glass, had gone when I met Rex. It was foggy, dark, and cold. I glanced sideways at him, at his flushed face, his heavy-lidded eyes. He was not like Mr. Hales, his talk did not come in an easy flow. He waited before answering, smiling that faint smile to himself, but when we were married, all his mind—what he really thought—would come out, each day would be an opening, a revelation.

"Rex, when are we going to be married?"

He was silent. His lids went down until his eyes were nearly closed.

"Rex?"

"A chap doesn't marry every girl he takes out."

I laughed. It was so funny. Everyone at the dance hall knew I was Rex's girl. He liked his little joke. He said things that were really quite stupid and managed to stop himself from smiling. I had only noticed it since I had been working with Mr. Hales.

"Where are we going?"

"To the pub, I s'pose."

"Let's go to another one."

"All right. One's the same as the other t' me."

"To Bincome."

"No, we'll go in the other direction, out Tanninghall way."

The room with the bar was warm and pleasant. I sat in a corner behind a small round table and he brought me a shandy. A little middle-aged pink-faced woman was behind the bar, and he did not lean over and talk to her as he usually did the barmaids, but went along and joined a group of men at the far end. He evidently knew some of them, as there was laughing and talking. The little woman polished glasses and watched me. She wore spectacles and they glinted. When I looked straight at her, she smiled. I sipped the drink slowly to make it last. I felt daring, sophisticated, with the feeling I always had, that it was naughty, wicked, to sit in a pub. I tried to look like a film star in disguise.

Two middle-aged men came in noisily, awkwardly, getting their bulk through the door. A greyhound slunk at their heels. They got their beer and carried it sloshing to the table opposite to mine. The one facing me had a big stomach and a check waistcoat. His face had grey bristles and, as he drank, his bloodshot bulbous eyes looked at me over the mug. He seemed familiar. I had seen him before. Yes, he was the vet who had come to our farm. I kept my eyes down. The dog came and put its nose softly on my knee. I smoothed the fawn bony head.

"Dolf!"

It slunk back and lay in the space between us, its ribs a cage, the haunches a saddle behind.

The vet leaned over and said something in a whisper to the man who had his back to me. He looked over his shoulder but turned quickly when he saw me watching. I had finished the drink. I studied the old fireplace intently, the horse brasses with minute care. I made up my mind to get up and stroll across and look at the notice in the far corner. I gathered my gloves, my bag, but my legs were too shaky. Rex and some of the young men came along the counter laughing and got their glasses refilled. They called to the others: "What'll yer have?"

"Same agen."

The woman said something to Rex and glanced at me, but he did not look my way. Quiet settled down as before with talk and laughter coming from the far end, the two men sipping their beer reflectively and the woman meeting my eye and hers smiling through her glasses.

Then the vet got up.

"Again, Fred?"

"Thanks, George."

He leaned on the counter, his face near the woman's, talking. Then she was saying something and inclined her head to where Rex was laughing. The man came back to the table without looking at me.

Presently the woman lifted the flap in the counter and came across the floor. She's going to ask me if I want another drink. I can't sit here any longer without ordering another drink. I felt the hot blood rising in my face. I haven't any money. She was up to me—her shoes were brown leather with thick laces.

"Would you like to come into our living room, dear? You'd feel more comfortable." Why should I want to go into her living room?

"Thank you very much," I said.

The room was small and smelt of cooking. An old woman sat in an armchair in a corner, a crocheted antimacassar behind her head. A cat lay curled asleep on another armchair by the fireplace.

"Sit here, dear. I'll leave the door open in case they want to be served."

The old woman was looking at me, her mouth working up and down over bare red gums.

"Who's that?"

"Just a friend, Gran," she shouted. "Just a young friend! She's deaf," she said confidingly; "deaf as a post."

She sat on a high chair near the open door watching through the crack.

"How old are you, dear?" she said without looking at me.

"I'm nineteen."

"Oh, you don't look as old as that."

Mine was a rocking chair. I pushed gently with my feet. It was pleasant after sitting upright in the bar.

"Does your mother know you're here?"

What was it Rex had once said, "Does your mother know you're out?"

I laughed.

"She knows I'm out."

"Is that your boyfriend? The one you came with?"

"Yes."

Wasn't she nosy! I felt proud saying he was my boyfriend.

"Does he usually leave you like that?"

Whatever did she mean? He hadn't left me; he was still there. I didn't answer. I rocked in silence. The old woman watched, her chin going up and down, her hand resting on her upright knobbed cane.

"Who is she?"

"A friend, Gran, a friend!"

There was stamping from the bar, whistles and calls of "Service!"

The woman got up and went out. The clock ticked loudly. The cat yawned, stretched one front leg straight out, the claws extended, stood up and arched its back, then sprang down lightly and curled up on the hearth rug.

The old woman thumped her cane.

"Who are you?"

"I'm a friend." I got up. "I must be going now. Thank you very much. Good night."

I walked through the door, across the floor of the bar. The vet and his friend looked up and watched me. I opened the outside door. I was out in the cool night air. I got into the car. The fog had gone and there were bright stars in the sky. The sign swung gently, "The Rose and Crown." I watched the door, "Frederick Goodrum, licensed to sell tobacco." Soon it opened and the men poured out. They went to their cars, their bicycles.

"See you, then, Rex!"

"Right, Harry!"

He got in. He was there, warm, breathing. He started the car. We drove in silence. He stopped by the copse where my bicycle lay hidden. I waited for his arm, but he just sat smiling to himself, his hands on the wheel.

"Rex, when are we going to be married?"

"Well, you're certainly not backward in coming forward."

"Oh, don't be silly, Rex." I laughed and put my face on his arm. Of course we were going to be married. He just loved his jokes.

"Well, I'd better be getting along," he said.

"But it's early yet. It's only half-past ten."

"We've got a busy day tomorrow and the next day. I must get to bed."

"Oh, well, if you must—" I leaned over and kissed him on the cheek.

"See you tomorrow night then," I said.

"No, I shouldn't think I can make it tomorrow night, or Friday. Be working late. Better make it Saturday."

Poor Rex, working hard on the farm! One day I shall be able to help him. I squeezed his hand understandingly, putting my whole heart into it.

"Night, night," I said softly and kissed him again. I got out and watched him drive away.

Chapter 14

On the next evening, when I left the Mill House, I rode to see Iris Baltrop. My lamp lit the trees as I rounded the corner by Foxes Copse—he will be there, the dark car will be waiting, he will have come—but ahead, the long straight road was empty. A fine light spattering of snow lay on the dry grey surface and wispy sheets of white rushed terrified in front of me in the icy wind. Occasionally pieces lifted, broke from the drifted sides, and the granules hobbled frantically after, trying to keep up.

Iris's house looked warm, the windows bright squares. I turned the knob of the back door with my stiff hand and called "Co'ee, Iris." The kitchen was a blaze of colour. Mrs. Baltrop stood by the large red and white check-covered table. Her eyes flicked quickly from my beret, my damp hair, my old raincoat, my snow-edged shoes.

"Iris's dressing. Do you want to see her?"

"Yes, I thought—"

"Well, just for a minute. We're expecting guests in half an hour."

She was in evening dress. A pink fluffy apron was tied round her waist. Her arms, neck and back were thickly powdered, her face rouged, she wore red lipstick. Her auburn hair, brighter than when I had last seen it, was puffed high, and she smelt of the violets tucked into the purple stuff of her gown. She saw me looking at them.

"From Mrs. Wilkins' greenhouse," she said. "They keep a gardener. Iris will be down soon."

She was spooning cream onto a large trifle. Trays of wineglasses stood glimmering on the table and saucepans were simmering on the stove. Annie Hurren, from the cottage near our farm, stood awkwardly in the corner. She wore a large striped apron over her black. She grinned at me, flushing, crumbling the corner of the apron nervously.

Mrs. Baltrop twirled the cream with a fork.

"Annie's maid here now," she said. Annie winked at me and Mrs. Baltrop turned quickly.

"Go and change and don't stand there gawking. And when you come down, you can put out the glasses like I said."

She turned to the blue painted dresser, took a cigarette from her gold lamé bag, and bent again over the trifle.

"These girls—" the cigarette wobbled in her mouth as she talked—"but it's very difficult to get proper staff these days—" Large red cherries dropped at intervals onto the cream.

"I expect your mother finds that."

She cut tiny leaves of angelica on greaseproof paper.

"But now that you are at Mr. Hales, I suppose he *is* suited."

She did not look at me. She put two leaves, one on each side of a cherry.

"Yes, it's an engagement party. Mr. and Mrs. Wilkins are coming to dinner. Iris is engaged to Gerald."

Gerald Wilkins—in a flash of memory I saw him—the pale pimply youth she'd always laughed about. One of those who always hung by the door, who always had to be pushed forward from the door.

"She's older than he is," I said.

"Yes, that's a good thing. I'm a tiny bit older than my husband. It gives one control. Of course one has to give them a bit of rope, but control of the business is the great thing."

The door burst open and Annie came in. She had changed her apron to a little white one edged with a starched goffered frill. Her thin plaits were looped round in a bun and the white cap sat on the plateau above. She giggled.

"Now take the trays and put a small and a large glass by each place. Careful, set the door open before you start. We're having two wines," she said as Annie went out laden.

The cherries and leaves, like a bed of flowers, were in place. She dipped into a basin of blanched almonds and spiked them upright in the empty spaces.

"The Wilkins have two shops. Ironmongery. I expect you know."

An almond fell flat in the cream and she fished it out carefully.

"One over at Bincome."

The trifle was finished. She stood back and looked at it, her head on one side. The glass sparkled. It was a red-spotted water lily. She took off her apron.

"He's the only child," she said, turning to put the apron in the dresser drawer. She picked up a newspaper opened and folded to show a photograph and put it in front of me.

"We've been to a lot of social functions lately, with the Wilkins. This was taken at the police ball. The Wilkins believe in keeping on the right side of the law."

It was a large photograph over a short paragraph.

> Chief Constable toasted by police at ball given to mark his retirement after a long and distinguished career.

The grey-haired, fine, elderly figure was flanked by burly-looking men in evening dress and one girl. She had short-cropped fair hair and muscular arms. In the background the faces of the Baltrops and the Wilkins were just distinguishable between the heads of the crowd.

Iris came downstairs. Was it Iris? I hardly knew her. Although their colouring was different, she looked like her mother. She seemed fatter, matronly. Her dark-green low-backed dress was tight, her hair—

"I've had a perm!" She put up a hand and touched her long earrings. "Do you like it?"

Her eyes, when she saw me, had lit with a curious excitement. It was the same look that had lurked there at school, with the paper, all those years ago.

"Did you want to see me about anything special?"

"No, Rex is very busy, so I just thought—it was a chance."

Her eyes blazed.

"Then you'd better be going. I'll see you another night. They'll soon be here."

I turned.

"Yes, all right. I'll see you sometime."

"Come this way." She gripped my arm. "Come out by the front."

"But I left my bike by the back door."

"That doesn't matter. You can walk round."

She shut the door. We were alone in the dark hall.

"Why didn't you come to the dance at Bincome last night?"

Her face was nearly touching mine. Her breath still smelt. She waited.

"Oh, we went to the pub at Tanninghall. Then we had an early night. Rex wanted to get home to bed. He was tired."

"But he was there! He came in about eleven. He took

Jennifer Jackson home!"

"Oh, yes, I forgot. He said he was going. I didn't want to."

My mother was clearing the table as I went into the kitchen.

"Oh, it's you. We've just finished, but I can warm it up."

"I don't want anything."

"It's mutton and turnips and potatoes."

"I don't want it."

"Would you like an egg on toast? Or an omelette?"

"I don't want anything."

"It'll only take a minute."

"I don't want anything! I told you. I don't want anything!"

She took the things to the sink. I sat in the wooden armchair and watched her. She was grey. She seemed thinner, smaller. She washed the china and put it on the old draining board. Then she went through into the dairy, leaving the door open. The heavy churn tipped and the milk fell into the pail, a white stream, then she stood the pail on the table and strained it into jugs. She came back.

"Your father hasn't come in with the eggs yet." She bent, poking the fire, then rattled coal into the top from the hod.

"Why don't you keep still!" I said.

She half rose, clutching a chair. The other hand was on her chest.

"Why do you keep messing about! When I am at home, you just keep messing about. That's why I don't come home!"

She looked at me. Her eyes were dazed, her fingers splayed on her breast.

"I might as well be out. There's nothing at home! I'm going to bed."

Her faded eyes were wide on my face, unseeing, then they altered as though something had passed.

"Yes, go to bed and have an early night. I'll fill your bottle."

"I don't want a blinking bottle! I tell you I don't want it! All you do is fuss. It'll drive me crazy!"

The bedroom was cold, the candle a little flame of fire. The sheets were icy. I saw the dark warm car. I turned my face into the pillow. My body was drawn up with my crying, racked with each shuddering sob. I lay face downwards and my pain opened outwards, pressed against the bed. Something warm, hard, touched me, the old stone bottle. My mother stood there. Why doesn't she speak? Why doesn't she put her arms round me? Mother—help me—I can't tell you—Mother—I can't break through to you, Mother—don't leave me—don't go away from me—love me—Mother—

"You'll spoil your pretty face," she said.

The next day the frost had gone and it rained. I sat at the teatable with Mr. Hales and watched it pattering on the window and streaming down the glass. It was past the time for my leaving, but I was in no hurry.

"Perhaps I should get a taxi. A pity we have no phone. But I like to feel cut off from the world. It would have been convenient on an occasion like this."

"I'll wait a little. It'll probably hold up soon."

What did it matter? I had nowhere to go. He was buttering another bun, his eyes watching the plate. He had been serious today, and had disappeared for a long while into the study. I expect it had depressed him not being able to work.

"It's a pity you have to go at all," he said.

Well, I suppose it was, really. It did seem silly to cycle home in all that rain and come back again in the morning.

"Oh, I think it's holding up now. I'll get my things on."

He still looked at the plate. He said something. What was it?

"I'm sorry. I didn't hear."

"I suppose you wouldn't care to marry me."

It was so funny. He looked so miserable sitting there. I couldn't hurt his feelings.

"Yes, thank you very much," I said.

He looked quickly at my face and his mouth twisted into a funny kind of smile.

"Oh, give it some thought." He got up. "It's not like giving a dog a pat on the head."

The rain had stopped as I cycled home. It was brighter; there was even a little watery sunshine. I felt better. Quite excited. Not about marrying Mr. Hales. Of course I couldn't do that. I could easily tell him I'd changed my mind, but I could tell Rex! That was the trouble with Rex, he was too sure of me. He just knew that I was always there waiting for when he was ready to marry. But if he thought that he was going to lose me! I would lay it on really thick when I saw him tomorrow night, that I had decided, accepted— Wouldn't he grovel! And I would let myself, after his tears and pleadings, be persuaded. Oh—the long lovely road was waiting. I cycled faster and faster, my legs spinning.

I ate my tea. I ate the fat pork, the dumplings that I did not really want. I nursed this lovely secret. It was warm and flushed my face. My mother bent over the stove. This room—the stillness, the sameness—just for once I would waken it, drop something into the grey bubble—burst it.

"Mr. Hales has asked me to marry him," I said.

She turned, her face seemed to widen, the wrinkles stretching out and vanishing. Something lit behind her eyes.

"And you—?" She was still waiting.

"I said I would."

She crimsoned. She fell on her knees and clasped me and the chair.

"Oh, Ann, Ann dear. I'm so glad. I've been so worried. But I knew you would come to your senses. You won't regret it. I promise you you'll never regret it."

I couldn't sleep that night. I lay awake, dreaming. Tears were streaming down Rex's face. He had opened his eyes and I saw right into them, his sad lost eyes begging me to comfort them: Don't leave me, say you'll never leave me, we'll be married, say it, say it. I got up and went downstairs. I put some milk to heat and made myself some cocoa. The stove was still hot and the room was warm. I took the photograph of my mother down from the wall and looked at it by the candle. She was young, she was laughing. Her hair waved onto her shoulders. Her cheeks were full, her eyes shining. She wore a lace dress with a low neckline. It was a party dress. I put it back and looked at myself in the mirror over the mantelpiece. She was like me.

There was the sound of talking as I went up the stairs. I listened by the bedroom door.

"It isn't right." My father's voice was loud. "It's the same thing all over again, no good'll come of it, a young girl like that—"

"I don't care what you say. She's going to marry him and that's that. What's my life been? Tell me, what's my life been? And that Rex Armstrong"—so she had known, she had known all along—"what good's he to her? That's been all your fault. I'd have put a stop to it long ago. But no, she must be allowed to go out, do as she likes."

"You know why I said that. To forget the other. She couldn't sit at home here brooding. She wants company her own age."

"And that Armstrong and those Baltrops, are they your idea of the company she wants? When I think of the time when I was young, the people I used to know—"

"That's the trouble, you don't now. You shut yourself up after that other because of what people thought—"

"Well, she's not making the same mistake I made. You should thank God for that."

"You forget the good times, love, with all your trouble. But, a long while ago, we had some happy times. It's not right. An old man and a young girl. It's the same all over again. No good will come of it."

My father and mother were quarrelling. I had made them talk! But he needn't have worried. I was not going to marry Mr. Hales.

It was bright the next morning. The sun shone. I cycled along slowly, savouring my secret. Tonight I would see Rex. I would forgive Rex. What was it Mrs. Baltrop had said—"Of course one has to give them a bit of rope." I was early. I would go to the village shop and get him some cigarettes and a box of chocolates for my mother. I would have to tell her tonight—no, tomorrow. Sunday and the chocolates would make it better.

The door was ajar so the bell did not ring. It was dark where I stood. The light from the little window at the far end on the right-hand side fell behind the pamphlet-hung grid where Mrs. Kerrison was sorting. I could just see her hands. A short square woman stood at the counter with her back to me. She wore a fawn mackintosh and a flat hat. Grey hair strayed untidily from a loose bun. On the wall facing her was an old mirror. Her face was reflected in it. I watched, fascinated. The mirror was framed in oak and at the top, in yellow, were the words "Gold Flake." At the sides were spots of blemish, tiny pinheads of black in radiating circles, like distended clusters of frogs' spawn. They drew her eyes up at the corners and her lip at one side. I thought she looked like the devil. When she talked, her teeth showed and her mouth was huge. I controlled my giggles.

"Yes, I've got stew for Bob's dinner today, so I was about betimes. I put it on and then I thought I'll get down there and back early."

Mrs. Kerrison didn't answer. She was counting under her breath.

"Well, have yer heard the news? That Rex Armstrong's cleared off. Went first thing this morning, so they say. Found things too hot for 'im, I shouldn't wonder. Got a girl into trouble out Bincome way, an' he'd bin carrying on with that Mrs. Mason, you know, her with th' red hair, dyed, I'd say. Her husband found out, so I've been told. An' then this girl Fielding—if her mother knew—that poor woman, all she's been through—they say she's got—" she leaned round to Mrs. Kerrison and her face was lost to the glass. She whispered something and then stood straight again and her face worked contorted in the mirror. "Oh, well, I always did say you never get rid of it. They never clear it right up. She's done everything for that girl. Now look at her. Old Williams, the vet, told my husband he saw them in a pub over at Tanninghall only the other night. Shameless hussy. How people come down in the world. I remember her people at the manse. You knew her grandfather, old Reverend Moore? A grand old gentleman, proud they were. Well, tha's a sure thing young people bring trouble on yer, though I must say our never had none with my George."

Mrs. Kerrison had come from behind the grid. Her round glasses, like small shining lamps, were focussed on me. The woman's mouth, stretched up at one side, still opened and shut.

"Well, he's gone now. Got a job up in Scotland, and good riddance, I say—"

Mrs. Kerrison did not speak. She still watched me, and the woman turned. She stared, mouth open. I had seen her, vaguely, somewhere before. Then she flushed and smiled.

"Oh, it's you. How do you like working for Mr. Hales, dear?"

The blood had drained from my body. It had left me numb, cold. Then something, a rod, slipped down my back. It drew me up. It stiffened me. I would show them.

Chapter 15

I am Mrs. Hales. I am Mrs. Bernard Hales. The moonlight filters onto the bed. The bars of the window frame are long, slanting on the carpet and reaching up to the pale counterpane. A bare tendril of the clematis taps gently. This morning I had been Ann Fielding, but now I am Mrs. Hales. I suppose I will have to call my . . . husband . . . Bernard. I can't call him Mr. Hales. Who was it called her husband Mr.? Mrs. Bennet—Fie, Mr. Bennet. There is warmth beside me, breathing. If I shut my eyes it is Rex, if I keep my eyes tight closed it is Rex—I am married to Rex and the moonlight is milky on our bed. My mother's eyes were shining because I had been married to Rex. There is movement beside me, arms, and I turn gladly to Rex. Two hands are cupped round my head, someone is looking at me, trying to force my eyes open.

"What is it behind your face? Some mystery. What are you thinking?"

The voice is not Rex's. It is not mine. Although it could have been always my thoughts spoken when I looked at Rex. Hands are on me gently like moths. Now a warmth is above me, pressing me down. Cold creeping gooseflesh prickles my body, and I stiffen straight with horror. A faint sweat, not my own, lays on my limbs. He is turning, trembling, away.

I felt I should never forget the look on Mrs. Baltrop's and Iris's faces. I had beaten Iris by a week. My wedding was in March, hers in April. She was living in the flat above the shop at Bincome. It did not compare in any way to the Mill House.

The March gale had howled across the marshes, flattening the grass and bending the reeds. It had flicked running ripples on the water as it rushed towards the weir. The snowdrops had clustered palely, low on the ground for shelter, and the catkins had hung helpless, shorn lambs' tails, in the wind. But now, in May, the noise had stopped and the grounds lay quiet, golden, shining in the sun. I was mistress of the house and I bustled about my housekeeping. In the evenings I helped Bernard catalogue his finds and then we had supper together. Occasionally I went to the loft above the coach house for apples which had kept well and were still hard and crisp. I looked from the window but I didn't see any more of Tom.

"Do you ever see him?" I asked Bernard.

"Never face to face, but I occasionally hear a rustle in

the bushes. I thought I saw him fishing once, but it may have been a shadow in the dusk."

"I'm going to write him a note. After all, we've had no quarrel with him."

"He can't read."

"He'll take it to Mrs. Kerrison. You remember how pleased he was with the note from Mr. Montague. Poor old man. *We* don't mind him being there."

I packed a few eggs in a basket. If he answered the door, of course there would be no need for the note, but I didn't think he would.

> Dear Tom,
>
> You remember Ann Fielding who stayed at the Mill House before Mr. Montague died? I am now Mrs. Hales and my husband and I would be very pleased if you would use the grounds as you wish and fish whenever you like.

I opened the little front gate. The pebble path had been taken up and there was now clipped grass, soft to the feet. In the long narrow beds by the sides hyacinths were pushing through, creamy green cones freshly peeled, and among splashes of red primrose fat white button daisies were thick-stalked, sturdy, above the low-spread crinkled leaves.

I stood on the worn brick step and lifted the little black knocker. The sound died away and there was silence. I walked round to the back. Did I fancy it? Or did the door shut hurriedly? The garden had been freshly planted. The wigwam of sticks was ready for the runner beans. The green tops of the shallots were already bending over in their tallness. I knocked on the door with my knuckles. There was no answer. I put the eggs down and walked again round to the front. I lifted the black ring and waited. Where the rockery had been in the corner, there were three rosebushes. I looked up at the little stone doorway. It was pitted and carved to a point at the top.

There was deep silence. Someone was watching me. I could feel their presence, their eyes. I pulled the flap of the letter box and slipped the note through, then I stood again, holding my breath, listening. The feather touched my cheek. The softness that I had felt in the loft caressed my face, my bare arm. I turned and ran. Beyond the gate, Bernard was coming across the grass. I rushed towards him.

Iris came to tea. The day before, I had raided the cupboards in the dining room and found them packed with silver. I cleaned dishes for the cakes and bread and butter, a cream jug, sugar basin, little claw tongs, and a teapot shaped like a boat. In the drawers full of linen, I found a white damask tablecloth, scalloped and embroidered with fine white roses, and little napkins to match, each with its central rose. I had a recipe book from my mother and I made a cake with icing, cut sandwiches, and had strawberry jam in a cut-glass pot. We sat, Iris opposite to me and Bernard between, at a round table in the drawing room by the window. The sunlight was hot on my arm and glinted the red of the jam. Bernard handed the bread and butter and cut the cake while I poured the tea. He smiled at Iris.

"Your husband should have come. Does he like to fish?"

"Oh, no, he's too busy. He doesn't mind a game of darts."

Iris was different. She flushed when Bernard looked at her and put on a funny kind of voice.

"I expect you are a great help to him."

"We're buying a car next week. We've got a van too. I'm going to learn to drive."

Bernard took her cup and passed it to me.

"That will be pleasant for you."

"Of course his father has got a van, and a car, at our other business. That'll make two cars and two vans."

"Oh, I can see that you are able to get about. Sometimes I think that Ann should have a car."

"Well, I know I'd want one if I was stuck here."

Iris was sweating. The moisture stood on her forehead, and the flush was on her neck in a red stain. Bernard wiped his mouth with his napkin and smiled at me.

"If you two ladies will excuse me—" He got up with his hand on my chair. "I will finish a little job I was doing." His hand pressed lightly on my shoulder. "I will leave you to show Iris round."

Iris watched the door close. Her flush had gone. "I say!

However you can stand it! It's like being married to your father."

"I never think of it like that. He's very kind."

"Oh, we all know why you married him, because Rex Armstrong went away."

She was walking round looking at the walls.

"Have you done your spring cleaning yet? I've started. I'm getting it all just how I want it. Come on, let's go and see the rest."

We went up the stone staircase.

"I say, why don't you have carpet on here? Fancy having a bare staircase! And all those old pictures, I'd clear them away and paper the walls."

"Bernard wouldn't like that."

"What's it got to do with him! You're mistress in your own house, aren't you?"

The door of the secret room was locked. We looked into Bernard's old room, with its dim-coloured rugs, the books with their leather bindings, the brown velvet curtains, the Chinese quilt, and the pictures on the walls.

"This is our room."

I turned the large china knob on the heavy door. The sunlight streamed across the pale blue carpet onto the wide bed. Over the white mantelpiece the girl looked at me, smiling. It was a painting in a carved frame. It was of delicate pinks, gold, and blues. The girl, naked, rosy from bathing in the sunlit pool, stood sideways looking over her shoulder, a mist of blue wrap in her outspread arms.

"I say! Isn't that disgusting! I wouldn't have it in the house!"

The girl smiled at me behind Iris's back.

Iris was looking at the wide bed, her eyes round. Men's silver-backed hairbrushes lay on the chest by the wall.

"Do you mean to say you actually sleep with him! You actually go to bed with him!"

"Well, we are married, aren't we? Don't you sleep with your husband?"

"That's different. An old man like that."

I felt a flash of anger. I felt sick, talking about Bernard. I wanted to get Iris out of the house.

"Come on," I said, "I'll cycle part of the way with you and get back while it's still light."

"Yes, I should clear all these old pictures away." She halted on the stairs and looked upwards to the high ceiling. "I should get busy brightening the place up."

"What's that noise?" she said as we went to get our bicycles.

"That's the weir."

"Do you mean to say it goes on all the time?"

"Yes, I don't notice it. I've got used to it."

"It would craze me. However you can live here—after all that other—don't you ever think about it? Don't you—"

Did I—Miranda?

We cycled along in the still bright early evening. I hadn't shown Iris the mill pool, I hadn't shown her Tom's cottage, I hadn't shown her the river, the orchards, the summerhouse, the coach house, the loft, the roses, the terraces with the pinky brick steps. But I felt relaxed, comfortable. I'd had Iris to tea and I'd got it over with.

We were halfway to Bincome.

"I'd better leave you now."

"Oh, don't be silly. You can come further than this. You can come right back with me and I'll show you what we've been doing."

"But it'll be dark before I get back."

"What's the matter with you? You've got lights, haven't you? You never used to mind the dark."

She gave me a sideways look.

"Not before you were married."

It was different then, with the black car waiting. She unlocked the door of the shop. It was dark inside.

"We close at five. Gerald has gone over to Bampton to see his father about the accounts. He'll be back soon."

We went up a narrow steep staircase.

"Of course we haven't finished things yet. We're having red carpet on here."

"It'll show every mark. My mother used to say patterned was best."

"Oh, well, you have to put up with that if you want to be smart."

The flat was just like her mother's house—the pink bathroom, the standard lamps, the cocktail cabinet.

"That was Mum and Dad's present."

"It's lovely, Iris; it really is all lovely."

Two chests of drawers, one by each wall, stood in the lounge. They were bright blue, with white edgings and black knobs.

"Gerald did these. They were old ones of his mother's. He scraped them right down to the bare wood and then gave them two coats of paint."

I touched them with a finger. They were so bright and glossy.

"You ought to do those old things in your lounge like that. All those cracks. I didn't like to say anything, but they could do with a coat of paint."

"Do you think I could? Do you think I could manage it? I've never painted anything before."

" 'Course you could. It's easy once you get a start. The preparation's the great thing. Gerald always says the preparation's the great thing."

"I think I will. I think I'll start tomorrow."

"We can let you have the things. Although we're closed, we can let you have them now if you like."

"Could you? Then I must be going. I'll see Gerald another time."

We went down and fudged around in the shop. It was exciting. I bought a little bright scraper like a three-pointed star, two grades of emery paper, a screwdriver, a large tin of undercoat, a tin of blue gloss, and some little black knobs.

"I think I'll do them exactly like yours. Yours look so nice."

"I'll lend you a bag. If you haven't enough, you can always come back for more."

I cycled home, the bag lumping against my knees. It was dark. The trees were massed black against the sky. I rounded the corner by Foxes Copse, sudden panic at my heels. I pushed, my legs aching, along the familiar roads. There was no light at the front of the Mill House. I hid the bag in the shed behind my bicycle. My heart was beating. I was late. Bernard would be angry. I opened the door.

The warm safe glow met my eyes. He stood, a little saucepan in his hand, smiling at me quizzically.

"I saw your light, so I made the cocoa immediately."

Two steaming mugs stood on the table. There were crusty rounds of bread, butter, cheese, and little red radishes in a jar.

"I'm sorry about your supper," I said.

"Oh, think nothing of it. I'm very domesticated. I expect you're worn out."

We looked at each other and we both laughed. I sat down near him at the table and stretched my legs. Then I turned and nuzzled my head briefly in the hollow of his neck above the shoulder.

I got busy the next morning. Bernard had gone to do his daily stint at the mound and I had the house to myself. I took the bag to the drawing room and laid thick newspapers on the floor, then I edged the chest forward from the wall. It had shabby mouldings of plaster round the edges, the gilt chipped here and there. It was a cupboard, really, with curved doors and little drawers underneath. There was a marble top, horrible, like a washstand, but I didn't know what I could do about that.

I unscrewed the handles. They were thin silly little brass things and two of them broke, then I got to work with the scraper and the moulding chipped away. All day I worked, locking the door when I stopped to get our light lunch. The faded flowers on the curved doors and the ridges where the legs fluted down were difficult. The flowers became brighter as I rubbed, and then they vanished and underneath was some thin brass stuff which floated onto the newspaper in little gold leaves.

At last it was done, down to the bare wood. There were still traces of cream in the ridges on the legs, but the paint would cover them.

The next day I put on the white undercoat, and on the third day, the blue gloss. It looked lovely. The white lines were very slightly wavy, but they didn't really show and the little black knobs looked so much better than those old brass things. Now I had started, I could do all the others. With a mounting wave of excitement I went to call Bernard. He came from the kitchen rubbing his hands.

"What's all this? What's this dark secret?"

He stood looking at it, smiling.

"Oh, I suppose this is something for the kitchen. But why do it in here? I know"—he held up his hand as I started to speak—"so that you could lock the door. Still,

I see that you've well protected the carpet. Where's the other?"

He looked around.

"The other—?"

"The commode that stood here. Where've you put it?"

"It is the one."

"It is—"

"I've scraped it. I got right down to the bare wood. The preparation is the great thing, Gerald said."

I looked at him, smiling. At last I had done something all on my own that I was proud of. He was looking at the floor, at the bits of gilt-chipped plaster.

"I haven't cleared up yet. I'm going to do the other."

His face had gone white. His cheekbones, his face, looked squarer, as though his teeth were clenched. Something twitched near his eye.

"You stupid—ignorant—little fool."

He did not look at me. He was different. Tears welled at the back of my eyes. Then he started to laugh. He leaned, his back to me, over a chair and laughed and laughed.

"To have survived Josephine's court and to have come to this!"

His shoulders were shaking.

"The courtesan demoted to the kitchen maid."

His laughter died suddenly and he turned and looked at me. I could feel the tears running down my cheeks and tasting salty in my mouth. He stepped forward quickly and put his arm round my shoulders.

"Come along. Let's go into the kitchen and make some coffee."

He rattled cups and I put my head on my arms on the table and sobbed.

"Come along. Drink it up. You'll feel better."

He pushed the coffee into my hand.

"I'm sorry. Of course you've a perfect right to do as you like. It's just that—" he smiled and spread his hands—"couldn't you leave things just as they are, just for a little? I'm an old man and when I'm gone, you'll still be young—"

"Oh, don't say that. Don't talk about it—"

"And why not—why are people so silly about dying? What is it—we are not that important. Why does it worry us?"

I was thinking of the other chest. I supposed I wouldn't be able to do it now.

"It was just that I thought the lounge wanted brightening up."

"The drawing room. Only pubs have lounges."

"Oh, no. Iris Baltrop—and Mrs. Baltrop—have got lounges, and pink toilets."

He frowned.

"A water closet, a lavatory, is not a toilet. One's toilet is the process of dressing, washing, attending to one's person. Oh, it's so stupid—" he spread his hands, frowning—"the covering up with embarrassed gentility of a perfectly natural function." He turned impatiently. "Oh, what does it matter. Just leave things as they are for the time being. By the time I am gone, I hope your ideas will have altered, but if they haven't, I'll leave an address to which you can write. Don't put things in the village sale, and then you will have more than enough money to do anything you like—" he put his hand under my chin and lifted my face and suddenly smiled—"to paint purple stripes right up the stairs, if you like."

Chapter 16

It was hot summer. In the mornings a pearly box opened its doors and golden bejewelled light burst from its confines and flooded over the marshes, the gardens, the sparkling river. In the evenings it left reluctantly, mischievous young streaks hiding in the sky until long misty arms reached out to get them.

I bathed in the mill pool after breakfast and Bernard waited to watch me before going to the mound. I splashed and laughed up at him as he hung over the bridge.

"Go along. I'm all right."

"No. It's not safe. The pool is very treacherous. I won't leave you here alone."

"But you couldn't save me. You can't swim."

"At least I could do something."

The sun was suddenly clouded over. The water was dark and green. I kicked my legs free from some weeds that entangled them. (I feel safe with Ann—I always feel that Ann would save me from drowning—is that not so, Ann?)

Sometimes, after, I put on my sun-baked dress and went to help him at the mound. He had removed the turf from a large portion, and, while the rooks cawed in the high trees, he scraped, brushed and sifted.

"Oh, really, however you have the patience! What do you hope to find?"

I suddenly saw clearly, under the huge mound, the tons of earth, a tiny skeleton lying right in the middle.

"It's something like those boxes," I laughed. "You'll open one and then another, and they'll get smaller and smaller and there'll be a little something in the last."

"At least I'm enjoying the journey. It's sometimes better to travel than to get there."

One evening at supper he had an air of suppressed excitement and after the things were cleared from the table and the lamp was lit, he lifted the heavy basket, put it between us, and removed the cloth. On the top of the grey fragments was a pair of gold earrings. They were round, conical, with long dangling fringes. He lifted one gently. The fringe fell over his fingers.

"Stroke it. Touch it. It has lain there for a thousand years."

He turned it over carefully.

"See, it has even a little clip for fastening, at the back."

He continued to stroke it, running his finger round the circular ridges of the cone.

"Think what has happened in the world while it has

been in the dark and quiet for a thousand years."

He lifted a stone-pointed prong from the basket.

"This also. Probably for the hair. Someone, perhaps, piled the hair high, put on the earrings, and went to meet her lover."

The gold fringe fell like water between his fingers.

"Who was she? What was she like? Now dead for a thousand years."

He spoke quietly as though to himself, stroking the gold.

"Laid with her belongings, at rest, in peace, for all eternity. Until some robber, some plunderer, some curious poker, breaks the ancient privacy. Sometimes I feel dirty, rattish, a burrowing peeping Tom. After what period of time does a violator of tombs become an archaeologist? Will someone turn our bones and call us a specimen?"

He laughed and his eyes suddenly looked up under his brows.

"Don't you realize that I really *am* a criminal? These are treasure-trove—treasure-trove. But I shall keep them —and hide them—just for a little. In my will I shall declare all and leave you to take the consequences."

He put his hands one each side of my head and turned my face to him. He often did this; it was very irritating. He did it mostly at night, and then he would force my eyes to look at him, and talk a lot of nonsense.

"You have the face of the young Ionian woman, one of the idols of a still uncultured Athens. A brooding mystery. What are you thinking? Is there emptiness? Or what are you hiding? Would you like to come with me to Greece? It is the one place for which I would leave the Mill House for a short while."

Go to Greece! Leave the Mill House! What nonsense was he talking? How could I leave the Mill House? Suppose Rex came back and I was not there? Suppose . . . Oh, what nonsense! Why couldn't he be quiet and leave things as they were?

"Greece—a land of blue sky, darker blue sea, and snow-white forms, a perfect higher parallel world of light and marble. I must show you the Acropolis, the Parthenon, the Lions of Delos. And yet there is a mystery. Only *we* now see this beauty as *we* imagine the architects conceived it, this perfection wrung from the higher reaches of the mind. Originally it was daubed with paint of a gaudiness, a crudeness beyond perception."

He was looking into my eyes, searching, as though he would find the answer there.

"Was it something to do with their religion, their sacrificial rites? The minds that could correct the optical illusion that makes horizontal lines sink and vertical lines bend, did they, to please the populace, concede instead of raising them to their heights? And yet I can understand. The razor sharpness is uncomfortable. One has seen. One has been there. What does it matter? To sink back to the commonplace. It is more comfortable."

I wrenched my face away. I wished he wouldn't run on so. I liked being married. I liked being at the Mill House and doing as I liked. I enjoyed the bathing, the cooking, the seeing to the house. I didn't even mind the sorting and cataloguing of the old grey stones, but I didn't like the nights. He usually talked like this in the bedroom at night. Whereas I would have given anything for Rex to have talked, I wished Bernard wouldn't. I wanted to lie quiet in the wide bed in the moonlight and dream of Rex. To dream that Rex was coming back. I was walking along a long straight road and there was Rex coming towards me. I wanted to be alone.

"Wouldn't you rather sleep in your old bed?" I said.

He looked at me for a long time. Then he spread his hands and gave his funny sort of smile. "It seems my caravan starts for the dawn of nothing—"

"Oh, don't be silly. You haven't got a caravan."

He did not smile. He sat looking at me, thinking, then, "Why did you marry me?"

I laughed. "So that I didn't have to go home in the rain."

"I wish it were wit, but I don't think it is."

I laughed and put my hand over his. "Why did you marry *me?*"

"Because you were young, warm, and—alive. I was afraid of losing your company."

"But you haven't. You won't. I love being with you. The old nights won't make any difference."

I lay alone in the half light of the moon, in the wide bed, as I had imagined. I watched the girl over the fireplace. She smiled, looking over her shoulder. I tried to dream of

Rex, but he would not come. For the first time for months, I noticed the sound of the weir. It was roaring, the water rushing towards the mill pool. It never stopped. If I closed my eyes, if I let go, I would be carried along with it. It would lift me and take me and slide me over the fall and I would be sucked deep into the dank green bottomless depths of the pool.

I could not sleep. I felt uneasy. I got up and went to the window. Little clouds were scudding across the moon. It was fading from the full and one side was fragmented, mushy, as though crumbling. The yuccas in their shining spears caught the light like little bells, but the bushes round were black and solid. Far across to the left were the trees surrounding Tom's cottage, and to the right, across the lawn, the open front of the old summerhouse. A dark cloud was approaching the moon. Its mass had blurred the clean line of the half circle and, just before the light was shut off, I saw a man with a fishing rod walk across the grass. There was a quick flash of silver on the fish dangling from his hand, and then darkness. It did not look like Tom. Someone was trespassing. I felt suddenly cold, with mounting panic. The feather touched my cheek. Then something soft was on my shoulders, my arms, as though the girl had stepped down and put her wrap about me. I tried to scream with rising terror, but no sound came. I wanted to run out, along the passage, and hammer sobbing on Bernard's door, but my feet would not move. Then I stumbled, fell upon the bed, pulled the safe covers over me, and lay quivering.

It was my birthday. On the day before there had been the excitement of mystery. It had been suggested, oh, so cunningly, that I cycle to see my mother and father. When I came home, the door of the drawing room was locked. I felt a falling of the heart. What had I wished for, in all the world, for my birthday? A horse? A car? At breakfast there were cards—from Iris, my mother and father—a bunch of red roses from Bernard. Then, "Follow me," he said.

The door was unlocked and opened with a flourish. By the French window stood a huge black piano. It was not tall. It was low and squat and shaped like a fiddle. It had three carved legs. A stool was covered with pale green brocade. Bernard watched my face.

"It was your mother's idea. I asked her advice. See, she has sent all your music."

I flushed. I felt the warmth rising in my cheeks. I stopped myself from crying.

"You like it? It is what you wanted?"

I went over to it and he helped me lift the shining lid. I touched a few notes with one finger.

"It's lovely. Thank you," I said.

My father died in the late summer. One morning my mother woke to find him dead beside her, and in the autumn Bernard fetched my mother to the Mill House. A large front bedroom was prepared and a nurse installed in the dressing room. My mother was in great pain. She was dying of cancer. A woman came from the village during the day to help me, and fires were kept burning in all the rooms to brighten the dark cold of early winter. I sat one night, by the shaded light, holding my mother's hand. She was shrivelled, tiny, in the bed. The nurse moved quickly, efficiently, around the room, straightening things, before she moved to her own door.

"Don't tire her too much," she said.

My mother watched my face, her eyes dark, sunken.

"Your father. It was lonely when he had gone."

The words were low. I bent over to hear them.

"We were happy. We were happy when you were little. I should have told him."

I smoothed the thin grey hair back from her damp forehead.

"Are you glad—glad that you married Mr. Hales?"

Was I? Rex—

"Yes."

"A good man—he's a good man—all he has done for me—"

She closed her eyes.

In the bitter January days her pain strengthened. It gripped her with savagery, and then she lay in a drugged sleep.

The nurse tapped on my door one night. My mother lay, her eyes open, her face relaxed, young. She grasped my hand and I bent over her. Her eyes searched my face. They wandered from my hair, my forehead, my every feature. Then they stared into mine with a strange intensity. They looked deep into me with a kind of pleading.

"I did," she said slowly, "have you taught to play the piano."

She died before morning.

I slipped into the room. The nurse was washing—preparing my mother's body.

"Perhaps you shouldn't—"

"Yes—she is my mother—"

Is—was . . .

A sheet was folded down from the waist. One limp breast hung. On the other side, where the breast should have been, was a large scar. I looked at it, my eyes dry, something rising and bursting in my chest.

"I didn't know."

She turned, her glasses glinting.

"You didn't know?"

"No. How long ago?"

"About six years. Yes, it was six years ago, in the winter. Just after that other"—she flushed and checked herself—"poor woman."

So there had been another reason why I had not gone home for half term. One perhaps that Miss Knight did not know.

"She never told me."

"You didn't know? You never guessed?" She smiled and touched my hand.

"I shouldn't worry. Don't brood on it. Most people are only thinking about themselves."

(Love me—help me—hold me—Ann.)

Chapter 17

"Dashing away with the smoothing iron—dashing away with the smoothing iron—" I hummed under my breath as I flicked the shirt over on the white cloth. Outside, opposite to the window, under the hedge, daffodils flung and bent their golden trumpets to the tune trying to wake the dormant bluebells at their feet.

I had finished. I put the pile of linen over my arm and rushed up the stairs—pillowcases in the airing cupboard, socks, shirts, in Bernard's room. I pulled open the big bottom drawer of the bureau. The bureau was a huge piece of furniture that had been in his family for years and years, and of which he was very proud. A shaft of sunlight brought out dark red tones in the deep rich mahogany. The bottom drawer was kept for shirts, the middle one for socks and ties, and the little drawers were stuffed with documents. The lining paper was crumpled. I lifted the other shirts out to straighten it. It looked yellowish, grubby, the edges torn. I hesitated. I hadn't any lining paper, but newspaper would do. I ran downstairs to the study and got two sheets from those heavy tomes that plonked through the letter box every morning and which I never read. Then I fetched a duster, knelt on the bedroom floor, took out the old paper and, reaching, gave the drawer a good clean. Something rasped and tinkled under my cloth. It was a little key. It had been right at the back in a corner under the old lining. I laid it on the carpet, put the shirts neatly in, then straightened and looked at it. It was small and silver-bright. None of the drawers were locked. I tried it in their holes. It didn't fit. I pulled out the rests and let the big flap down. It didn't fit that either. A mass of letters, papers, manuscripts, tumbled forward, and at the back were lines of little drawers. They had no keyholes. I pulled the brass knobs but they would not move. They were all dummies. Then, right at the top of the stretch, I found a tiny keyhole. The key fitted. I turned, and the whole back, the whole flap with the dummy drawers, came forward and lay down. It was exciting. At the bottom were two rows of little drawers, but they were real. Above were cubbyholes and, in the centre, a little door. They all opened and were full of letters, sealing wax, drawing pins, and bits of string. Behind the little door was a pot of ink looking old and dried, and sticky labels and labels for tying. On each side of the door was a narrow strip of ribbed wood pannelling. On the right-hand side it jutted slightly forward at the top. I pulled it with my fingernail. It came out like a thin book from a bookshelf. It had an opening at the top. I turned it upside-down and tapped. It was empty. I put it back and looked at the other side. It was firmly fixed. It looked like part of the woodwork. I pulled with my fingernail. It did not move, but a speck of yellow stuff floated down. Glue, it had been glued along the top. I got one of the drawing pins, pressed it here and there, making little holes and scraped, pressing. Then, under the letters, I saw a little paperknife. It was better than the drawing pins. I stuck the point in, cut along the top, then prized the strip forward. It came out with a plop. It was like the other, but it wasn't empty, it was full of photographs.

I drew up a chair and sat comfortably at the bureau. This was exciting and pleasant. There was Bernard as a little boy. He had a round hat and a hoop. There was Bernard with two Labrador dogs, and Bernard, older, on a horse. There was Bernard with a man and a woman. I looked at the back. "With Mother and Father, 1888." He was like his mother. There was a photograph of a girl. It was a proper studio portrait. She had a long thin face and frizzy hair and a black velvet band around her throat. I stared at it. I had seen her somewhere before. I turned it over. "From Stephanie, with all my love, April, 1893." Where had I seen her? I picked up another. It was a snapshot. Two men, with a girl between them, were standing under leafy hanging trees. They each held a bicycle. The men had long plus fours, Norfolk jackets, and cloth caps, the peaks pulled forward over their eyes. The girl wore a long skirt which she was holding up at one side, a tight-fitted top, and a flat straw hat. They were laughing. It was the same girl. The man on the right was Bernard, and the man on the left—he was tall, very thin, and older—surely it was Mr. Montague? It couldn't be. He said he hadn't known Mr. Montague. I turned it over: "Stephanie and myself with R. Montague. Cambridge, 1894." I suddenly remembered where I had seen the girl before: with Miranda, when we had tried on all the old clothes in the bedroom and flung the windows wide. The photograph on the dressing table—she was Mr. Montague's first wife.

Silly old Bernard, why hadn't he told me? I ran downstairs, clutching the snapshot in my hand. I peeped, he was in the study, reading the paper. I felt warm and pleased with this secret. We would have lunch and then, while we had coffee, I would spring this surprise on him.

He fetched the pot from the stove and put it in front of me and I poured two cups. He looked at me, smiling, while he drank. I would wait until he had finished, then I would slap the snapshot down in front of him.

"I thought you told me that you didn't know Mr. Montague?" I would say.

The midday sun was shining in through the small window. It had not yet reached the pink bricks of the terrace where it would lay golden and creep into the kitchen by the open door.

Bernard turned, and the shadow of a bar of the window frame fell across his face. It looked different in profile, without the smiling stars of the eyes, the roundness. It was chunky, rough-cut, of a surprising jutting strength.

A sudden cold flash struck at me and froze the words on my mouth, an utterly unreasonable terror. When he turned again, I kept my eyes down and bit my lips to control a rising hysteria. I felt that there was a corner of the photograph sticking up in the opening of my blouse, but I dare not look, to draw attention, because if he saw it—some nameless horror: something inside me said, "Hold fast." I gradually controlled myself, and, with an adult strength I had never known before, I looked up into his face and smiled. We cleared the table and washed the few things and when he had gone, I rushed to the old tool shed to find glue. He must not know. I must put it back —my heart was hammering. I was frantic lest he should go upstairs and find the bureau open.

At last the photographs were in their old hiding place, the little compartment sealed again with glue. I locked the inner flap, closed the bureau, pushed the little key to the back corner of the shirt drawer under the paper, and sat down breathless.

Overriding all was a feeling of loss and utter loneliness. Bernard had been a warm hand holding me, so that I was still a little girl in a dream, but now the veil was ripped aside and my attention was forced around to my pain. I remembered what Bernard had said when I had always shied away from anything unpleasant. "You are still suffering from amnesia. Amnesia is a funny thing. Is it a chemical in the brain that shuts out intolerable things, or is it sent by God to cloud and soften the memory? As I get older, I prefer to think the latter."

But now I was sitting in this house and outside in the dank river someone had been murdered, and away in a prison yard someone had been hanged, because I had stood in a court and told what I saw. There had been only two possible suspects—Miranda and old Tom—but now a whole new aspect entered my mind. Why had Bernard come here, why had he said that he did not know Mr. Montague when evidently he had been on friendly terms, even affectionate terms, especially with Mr. Montague's first wife? Why had he taken such an interest in accounts of the trial that he had known me immediately?

In sudden fright as I sat on the bed, I reached and opened the drawer and pulled a freshly ironed shirt onto my knees as an excuse for being there in case Bernard entered the room—as though he could now climb the stairs silently, or had wings!

The absurdity struck me—how silly! The whole thing was silly! No doubt there was a perfectly ordinary explanation. Stephanie was the key. At tea I would find out how well he had known Stephanie.

I prepared the meal with special care and waited. Bernard was late. I strolled, after a time, to the mound, but it was deserted. Little terraces had been dug on two sides. It looked like a miniature pyramid, and at the back, untouched, the old nasturtiums still hung. Then, in my new awareness, for the first time I forced myself to the landing stage. I did not go on, but watched the water slosh, sloshing between the boards at the edge, and I turned in fright but no one was there. I went back along the brick terrace to the front of the house, to the great bush of yellow forsythia that grew by the front door. The stalks were tough and I fetched scissors and gathered an armful and mixed it with some of the daffodils that made a yellow carpet at its feet.

The sound of a car door banging made me look up. By the entrance gates someone in a fawn car was preparing to drive away. Bernard, with his back to me, was waving his hand in farewell. I slipped with my flowers round by the side of the house and into the kitchen. I breathlessly removed bulrushes and dried grasses from a tall blue and white jar and arranged my yellow glory in the sun. I stood the jar on the warm pink bricks in a corner against the white wall and sat down waiting. Bernard came in smiling.

"Sorry I'm late."

I waited for him to say, "Just seen so-and-so—" or "——called," but he did not. He was altered, I thought. He is playing a part. Well, so can I. Surfeited, more comfortable after the food and drink, I slipped, little girl fashion, to the floor and put my arms on his knees.

"I don't believe you love me any more," I said, looking up into his eyes.

"I was under the impression that you no longer loved me."

"Don't be silly. Tell me"—I played with his hand, looking down—"have you ever loved anyone else?"

"Why do you ask?"

"I'd just like to know." I met his eyes coquettishly. "Don't you think I've a right to know?"

He looked away.

"I was engaged once. I suppose I should have told you."

"What was her name?"

"Stephanie."

My knees were suddenly weak on the hard floor. I lowered my eyes in case he should look down.

"What happened?" My voice was almost a whisper. "Why didn't you marry?"

"Someone took her away from me."

I looked up into his face. I need not have worried that he would notice me. He was alone, his face set, his eyes black with bitterness and hate.

I felt a shaft of jealousy for the long-dead Stephanie.

"You loved her very much?" My voice was almost inaudible, buried in my chest.

He gave a sudden jerk as though shaking himself. He lifted my chin with his finger and I saw that his face had cleared. He smiled.

"One gets over these things. Now I love you."

I got up, left everything on the table, and walked out. I went into the drawing room and sat at the piano. The sun had crept round and the golden light lay on the white keys, the black shining vastness. Open on the stand was the piece of music that I used to play over and over to Miss Mattocks. I suddenly, my mind running forward, heard again the crashing sea, the call of the gull, but it was just a jumble of notes. I could not wring it through my fingers from the piano. I touched a few keys and felt suddenly nervous of the noise dropping into the quiet room. Tears welled in my eyes, as though pretending, the deceit, had left me cold and alone. The door opened softly and I knew that a tall black shape stood behind me. I felt a shaft of fear. He came closer.

"You don't like the piano, do you?"

"No."

"You hate playing, don't you?"

"Yes."

"We must see what we can do. Go out tomorrow for the day, and we will see what we can do."

I rode, the next morning, in the clean crisp air. I passed our old farm. A strange man on a tractor was ploughing up the rough meadow by the road. I suddenly saw my father, walking behind old Dobbin, quietly carving the fields in autumn into clean, falling, bending slices. This iron monster ripped and roared, tearing with rage the soft green flesh that had thickened in centuries. I wanted to cry out as my buttercups and daisies, purple cuckoos and white stars of Bethlehem disappeared, bruised and cut, under suffocating brownness. I turned my face away. The birds were singing in Foxes Copse—Rex—don't let me think of him on this bright morning. Let me think of what surprise there would be for me at home. I knew what I wanted—but I dare not think, I would not think. I would go to see Iris. I hadn't seen the baby. Would it be like Iris or Gerald? Would its breath?—I started to giggle—would it have Iris's sharp nose and sallow skin?

The bell tinged as I went into the shop. Gerald, wearing

a grey coat overall, was serving a customer. He glanced at me.

"Iris?"

"Yes. Is she in?"

He waved a vague hand.

"Go right up."

The red stair carpet was dusty and littered with torn-off labels, pieces of string. Cardboard boxes stood at the side. Someone was rushing about behind the door. I knocked gently. There was a pause, quietness, then a clatter and another pause, then the door was half opened. Iris stood there. She had a saucepan in her hand, and her eyes were wide, startled, on my face.

"Oh, it's you."

"It's a lovely morning. I thought I'd pop over."

She still stood, the door half closed.

"Well"—she turned away—"I suppose you'd better come in."

A large pan full of nappies suddenly boiled over and spluttered on the stove. The wet steam rose and hovered, a white cloud, below the ceiling. Dirty linen filled the sink and crockery was stacked on the draining board.

"I suppose you're a lady of leisure now."

She stood with her back to me and, piling the linen out of the sink into a wicker basket, started to wash up. Her figure had thickened and dragged downwards. There were ladders in her stockings. Her hair was looped back with a slide and hung in greasy strands.

"How's the baby?"

"He's been crying all night. I've just got him off. He's in the bedroom."

"I'd like to see him."

"Well, you can't now. The least sound'll wake him."

I got up.

"Let me help. I can wipe."

"No, I'd rather do it myself. You don't know where things go."

"Can't I do something? Peel potatoes or do some of that washing?"

"No!" Her face flushed. "I tell you I'd rather do it myself!"

I sat down again. There was silence. Then my elbow knocked a brass ashtray off the corner of the table. It fell with a thud and circled with a loud clatter before it settled. Crying started behind the opposite door. It was a faint drawing in and letting go of breath, then it gathered force and became loud shrieking.

"Now look what's happened." She glanced wildly at the clock. "Gerald'll be in for dinner at one!"

"Shall I see if I can quieten him?"

"No! Let him shriek. Don't go near him. Oh, dear—"A tear stood in the corner of her eye.

"Perhaps, if I can't do anything, I'd better be going. I said I wouldn't be long."

Her face relaxed. She half smiled. The crying had stopped.

"Did you?" She edged to the door. "Well, I'd better be getting the dinner on. We've only got sausages. They won't take long—"

I stood awkwardly. "I'll see the baby another time."

"Yes. I'll let you know. I'll send a card. Perhaps one afternoon—"

"Yes—well, goodbye."

"Goodbye."

She shut the door behind me quickly, firmly. Gerald was busy with customers. He did not look up. Several people waited. I walked out.

The man and the tractor had gone from the field. There was flat emptiness. Even the birds were quiet in Foxes Copse. I called at the shop. I bought chocolate, tea and sugar. Mrs. Kerrison was alone.

"I sent Tom a note. Did he bring it to you to read?"

"No, I've seen nothing of it."

"How is he now?"

"Worse than ever. Allus comes after it gets dark."

I cycled back to the Mill House. It was early, but I had nowhere else to go. I went to the drawing room door. I stood for several minutes with my hand cupping the smooth knob, then I turned it quickly. The piano had gone. The sunlight shone on the pale carpet where the black mass had been. A note, a white card, was stuck prominently on a chair.

"Look in the coach house."

I ran out through the French window, along the terraces, across the gravelled yard. The sun shone full into the big high building, and there, on the old worn bricks, stood a little car. It was black, with a fawn hood, it had a little round snub nose. I stood, joy rising, a warm tide. I wanted to hold it, embrace it, hold my arms out to it. A long dark shadow lay on the bricks and went halfway up the whitewashed wall. It was Bernard. I turned and flung my arms around his neck.

Chapter 18

This must be Easter Monday—yes, I am sure that yesterday had been Easter Sunday. I had seen Easter eggs in the village shop and Mrs. Kerrison had said, "Easter is very late this year." I went into the study and looked at the large calendar—yes, today was Easter Monday. There was a forgetting at the Mill House of date and time—Bernard passionately engrossed at the mound, keeping in touch with the world through the dull pictureless papers that filled the wire letter box basket every morning—and I busy with the house, the garden, the specimens, the dreaming, the dream underlying all, that one day Rex would come back. This was pleasant, the sound of the weir, the rocks jeering, calling the world to wake, the primroses like clusters of newborn chicks nestling by the pool, but it was only temporary, it was only a waiting.

Easter Monday—bank holiday—I put my tea towel down, went outside and looked across the marshes. For some reason I thought of the horse that we had had when I was a child and the fair that had come once a year to the village. As the music of the roundabout had wafted across the fields the old horse had lifted its head, sniffed the air and listened. Then it had arched its neck and danced round and round, keeping in time to the march. It had probably been in the war, my father said.

Now as I looked across the marshes, there was silence —just the sound of the birds and the weir, but far away, across towns, roads, and bridges, there was music and laughter. I had gone, years and years ago, with some of the girls from school and their parents to the big seaside town, and we had ridden on the roundabout, swings, and a monster of a snakelike thing called a scenic railway.

I turned and ran with frantic haste up to my room. I stripped off my frock, my sandals, splashed my face and brushed my hair. Then I put on the Macclesfield silk dress, beige with a faint gold stripe, that Bernard had chosen for me, my white flat strapped shoes. I grabbed a handful of notes from my monthly allowance in the dressing table drawer, then dashed downstairs and wrote on a card, "Gone for a drive. Won't be late." With beating heart, I went to the car. I had had lessons from a curly-headed red-faced man from the garage at Bincome where Bernard had bought the car. We had gone to crossroads, backed, turned, backed again. I had driven through Bincome on Market Day. "And if you can do that, you can do anything," he'd grinned. Now, speeding along the road to the turnpike, the car was part of me, it was my legs, my horse, and, when I turned into the traffic, my enveloping bullet-nosed casing to drive through the busy crowds.

There was pine scent from the great stacks of timber by the river as I went towards the town. Huge white ships lolled, rocking. The sunlight sparkled on tips of little waves. Sea gulls waddled awkwardly, then rose, things of silver soaring grace, to drop again on the far bank and join a squawking group, quarrelling over rotting fish thrown out from the market.

The bridge was up. Round the corner, a solid block of traffic waited. There were ponies and carts, motorbikes, smart large cars, tiny shabby ones, people on bicycles and people walking. The bridge rose into the sky and the great ship came blaring. It passed with silent silken ease, and sailors leaned on rails and waved to small boys who hung from car windows, shouting. The bridge slowly fell and we streamed over towards the town. I drove to the big hotel on the Front. I felt hungry. I would have a meal and then explore. My feet sank into the soft carpet as the head-waiter looked up from the far end and came towards me.

I sat by the fireplace in the quiet dimness. I ordered chicken and a carafe of wine. The headwaiter watched me. At a table nearby were three elderly people—a man, two women, and a girl. The man sat facing me and he stared with a slightly puzzled frown. After several minutes I raised my eyes over my glass and his face had cleared, broken, as though he remembered something. He whispered to the others and they all turned to look at me, then turned hurriedly away.

I drank coffee in the huge lounge. The four people were some distance off. They were chatting with sudden animation, with occasional glances at me. The girl turned pages of magazines listlessly. I looked around. With the exception of the girl and myself, all the people were old. Some snoozed after their meal, others stared into space. The women were carefully coiffed. They wore rings. I wanted, suddenly, to cover the large winking diamonds on my left hand. The chandeliers, the thick carpets cloaked the silence. I rose, paid the bill and walked out. The noise, the colour, the shouts of laughter, the sunlight on the water, hit me with a blaze of gaiety. I went to the left, to the far end, then drove slowly down the Golden Mile. Hired horses and gigs, and phaetons, filled with laughing people mingled and clap-clapped on the tarmac. Gardens lay, bright with daffodils, primula, and hyacinths. Men in white straw hats bent, rolling their bowls, and younger people danced on tennis courts. To the right, cinemas, hippodromes, the greatest circus in the world, shouted their wares, and queues, like multi-coloured snakes, waited for whelks, winkles, sausages, and hot pease pies.

I stopped opposite to the Pleasure Beach. The scenic railway dipped, rushed, and rattled as I remembered it. The horses on the roundabouts went eternally up and down, flaring their dead nostrils. Girls and boys linked arms and walked in long lines, laughing. I paused by a shooting gallery and watched.

"Come on, one at a time. No pushin'."

Young men leaned importantly on their guns, then

looked behind to be sure that their girls were watching. A girl stood alone. She wore a short black skirt, a tight orange jumper. Earrings flashed from her ears and lipstick gashed her face.

"Come on, Flossie, what about you?" the man called.

"My name ain't Flossie."

"Well, Popsie then, what about one on the house?"

"I don't mind if I do. I'm good at most things."

They all roared with laughter. One poked the other.

"I bet she is."

They crowded round the girl as she leaned to shoot. One jogged her elbow and another slapped her across the buttocks. They all left together, the boys calling and shouting. I felt suddenly alone. Soon the booth was empty. The man glanced casually as he rubbed the barrels with an oily rag and hummed under his breath.

"I think I'll have a shot, please."

I fumbled in my bag. I had shot once, only once, years ago, at home, and then I had cried over the poor broken furry body. But this was different. This was just at fawn black ringed cards.

"Certainly, madam. Which gun would you like?"

Why did everyone talk to me differently? Why wasn't he jolly as he was with the other girl? She was about my age.

I remembered my father's advice. For a running target, aim your sights with a wide margin in front. Move your gun slowly and just before dead on, fire. For a fixed target, move your gun slowly upwards and just before sighting the bull, fire. I hit the bull with the first shot. The others pattered like daisy petals around the centre. The man took down the card almost reverently.

"Very good, madam. You're used to shooting. Which prize would you like? Anything on the third row."

There were garish ornaments, dolls with staring blue eyes and sprouting straw hair, golliwogs with black button eyes and red checked trousers. I didn't really want anything, but I didn't like to hurt his feelings.

"I'll have a comb, the brown one," I said hurriedly.

He gave it to me gravely.

Why was everyone so formal with me? Why didn't he laugh and joke as he did with the others? I would have my fortune told. I pushed my way through the mass of mothers, fathers, children holding sticky half-eaten rock, the paper falling back like the petals of pink daffodils. I slipped off my rings, put them in my pocket, and approached the tent of Madam Mawrica, Genuine Romany, Patronized by Royalty. She stood by the half-open flap and watched me come. I walked slowly, paused and read the notices, looked at the splayed hands with marked areas of territory, the hairless heads divided into planes.

"Tell yer fortune, lady."

I hesitated, teasingly, considering.

"Half a crown one hand, five shillings for two."

"Yes. All right."

She seemed surprised. The interior was close, heavy, lit by a guttering candle standing on a small central table. A thick Oriental rug covered the uneven sand, and a large black cat stared, its green eyes slits, from a heap of rags in the corner.

"One hand or two, dear? Or you can have the crystal for ten shillings."

"Two hands, please."

"The crystal's best, dear. I can tell more by the crystal."

"Two hands, please."

She settled herself. Multi-coloured drapery, like an Indian tablecloth, fell from her head and wrapped her in folds. Gold earrings glimmered from under her straight dark greasy hair, and turquoise, coral, and emerald beads hung to her waist. Her black eyes flicked over my dress. One hand, a thin brown talon, suddenly shot out and fingered my bag as it lay on the table, the soft cream suede bag that Bernard had given me, with its golden clasp.

"A nice bit of leather that, dear."

Then she peered at my outstretched palms.

"You have rich parents. You were born with a silver spoon in your mouth—"

She spoke automatically, as though reciting. She smelt musky, like the spice my mother used to put in the gingerbread.

"You have never known what it is to be poor."

She turned to the other hand.

"You have always lived a quiet life. You have had no troubles."

There was quietness, then she suddenly opened a box on the table and took out a cigarette.

"D'yer mind if I smoke, dear? It helps the concentration."

She turned again to my palm.

"Do you do anything special, dear? Dance or play the piano?"

"Yes."

"You will achieve your heart's desire. You will be a great musician."

"Will I marry?"

My heart beat waiting. Rex . . .

"I can't tell you that, dear, unless you have the crystal. Will you have the crystal?"

"Yes."

She removed a black cloth and the orb glimmered in the candlelight. Her lean hands, like two bats, shaded her face. Her voice was slow, different.

"I see water. Green water. I see a man—yes—I see a man—"

"What is he like?"

"He is tall and thin—he has grey hair—"

"He is old?"

"Yes—he is holding out his arms to you—"

Who could that be? It wasn't Bernard, it wasn't Rex.

"What is he like?" I asked again.

"I can't see, dear—the water is swirling—and you are running—you are running from him—"

She put down her hands and covered the crystal.

"That's all I can tell you, dear. That'll be fifteen shillings."

She watched as I counted out the money.

I turned to go. "You didn't see if I was going to be married."

"No. Has your house water by it?"

"Yes."

I looked over my shoulder. She was still watching me. Silly old woman, she had been wrong about everything.

I passed the booth with the largest rat in the world, the hairy lady, the fat lady, the ghost train. Couples were waiting to enter the tunnel of love. I went into the Hall of Mirrors. Three girls and boys were chasing each other. They screamed and barged about, calling.

"Look what you're doin', Ted," one shouted. "You'll break the bloody glass."

They knocked into me and I laughed, but they took no notice. Then they looked at themselves, at their great bodies and tiny heads, their huge heads and long sticklike legs. They stuck out their tongues and put their hands flapping from their ears. They contorted to get their legs to the top and their heads to the bottom. They screamed, rocking with laughter. One mirror was almost normal, slightly wavy, and a girl stood behind me. She was my height, the same age, but I was different. It was my clothes. It was my clothes that altered everything and made me different. I left the Pleasure Beach and walked along the Front. Young people walked with linked arms, laughing. Some wore paper hats and had silly notices pinned to their chests. A girl in a bathing costume, clinging tightly to her leather-coated swain, roared by on the pillion of a motorbike. Cars passed slowly with boys and girls spilling out in their bright colours, sitting on bonnets, standing and waving rattles. I watched, an ache in my throat.

I returned to the car and drove slowly back along the Front until I had left the noise and the laughter behind. I went to the far end where the road narrowed and went off to quietness around the coast. Then I reversed and stopped among a line of parked vehicles. I wanted to think, to ponder on the events of the weeks before, but I could not. To my left on the far side of the wide path were sand dunes and then the sea. The dry sand was piled in little waves and hills like the desert and, beyond, the sea sparkled like a vast oasis. To the right, across the road, quiet substantial houses stood well back, some bearing the discreet card, "Bed and Breakfast."

A fawn car was coming along the road in front of me. It stopped on the other side about four houses down. It was vaguely familiar, which was funny, considering I knew so few people with cars. The door opened and a woman got out from the driving seat. She was about thirty-five, with close-cut, shingled, rather rough fair hair, and I saw that she was lame. She went round to the gate of a grey stone house and Bernard got out of the car on the other side. They went up the short path together, entered the house and closed the door. No, it could not have been Bernard, whom I had left at home in old clay-covered clothes working at the mound. But it was—there was no mistaking him—and the car was the one I had seen at the gate.

I started the engine numbly, automatically. I turned round in the road. I could not go forward past the house in case they should see—be looking. I drove again until I came to the end of the Front and turned left. I must keep turning left to circle behind the town until I came to the bridge. I passed rows and rows of tiny houses, warehouses, great yards with their own little shunting railways. At last there were throngs of people, the market with the cockle stalls, the ice cream stalls, the brightly coloured fruit, the smell of fish and chips. I turned right to the honk of a ship and there was the great white bridge. I was over, I was out of the town onto a familiar road. My panic gradually subsided. How silly it was—why should I expect Bernard, with so many more years and experience than my own, to have nothing whatever apart from me? She might be an archaeologist or even a lady solicitor—yes, that was probably it—he was making his will and did not care to mention it. On bank holiday? I must put it away from me, I must not think of it.

I started to hum, driving was so enjoyable. The Mill House came into view all too soon. Poor old Tom, his cottage looked so lonely. Now, how pleasant, wouldn't it be, if I could just call, have a chat about old times, because after all we were the only two left that knew, the only two — But no, it would be no use, it would be as it was before —the knock on the door, the listening, the silence, perhaps even the familiar panic.

I let myself into the Mill House with the key that I always carried but had never used. How comfortable it was to be home. I grilled some steak and had hot strong coffee. I felt better. It had turned chilly. I riddled the kitchen stove and the glowing fire was pleasant. The clock ticked loudly and gradually the window darkened and it grew dusk. The loop was off Bernard's old coat and surely the peg, as it hung on the kitchen door, would soon be poking a hole in the back. I had been meaning to mend it for ages and now was the chance. I spread it on my knees and threaded the needle. There—did anything else want doing? I turned out the pockets. A tightly folded wad of paper was in the right-hand side. I opened it out. It was the middle sheet from one of the heavy newspapers that dropped through the letter box daily, and was a week old. At the top of an article was a large headline, "The Case for the Abolition of Hanging," and in the centre was a photograph of Mr. Montague. It was strange seeing it in the paper. There had been no photographs of Mr. Montague in the other papers long ago. I remembered this one. It had been taken by Miranda with her old box Brownie and was very good. He stood tall and straight, looking at the camera, slightly contemptuous, because he had been rather annoyed at our long laughing and "non'acking" about.

I folded the paper tightly again, in exactly—exactly—(sudden panic seized me) the same folds. Bernard must not know—must not know—I had looked at the paper. He must not know I had mended—I seized the scissors, tears starting from my eyes, my hands shaking. I plucked at the threads, pulled off the loop and hung it over the peg.

Before he got home, I must get to bed and lock my door. I ran, his key would rattle any minute, seized a book from the shelf in the hall, and was safely locked in my room. Locked away from Bernard—how strange—I lay reading. It was *Pride and Prejudice* by Jane Austen. I had read it three times before. I listened for the sound of a car. Even if a car or taxi didn't come to the door, I should hear it on the road. But there was just the sound of the weir. Then suddenly—my heart leaped—there was the click of his key in the lock, and the big front door being pushed open. His footsteps sounded on the stairs. They paused by my room and I held my breath—then his bedroom door softly shut.

How had Bernard returned home? There had been no sound of a car.

I woke, still sitting up in bed, my book dropped to one side, my arms cold, held stiffly. Moonlight streamed into the room, showing plainly the time on the little gilt clock on the mantelpiece—a quarter to three. I got out of bed to draw the curtains and looked at the ghostly white world. Everything was deathly still. No breeze stirred the bushes, the pink froth of cherry blossom, even the leaves on the trees were rigid in sleep. Then suddenly, in a thin slit of moonlight, in the dark shrubbery, there was movement. The woman stepped out into the open. She wore a light coat that matched her hair and by her chest she was holding something steely black. Was it . . . a gun?

I waited until she turned her back, then I drew the curtains and climbed back into bed. I snuggled down into the warm darkness.

"Oh, Lord," I whispered, "keep me safe."

Chapter 19

The gooseberries were difficult to gather. They hung like green grapes at the bottom of the bushes through a fretwork of branches. The thorns pricked my fingers. My back ached, but there—I had finished. I would sit on the grass under the big oak and top and tail them for jam and then go to Mrs. Kerrison's for sugar. I straightened. No, I would go now. I was sick of gooseberries for a while.

Blossom twined in the tall green hedge to my left as I walked along. Convolvulus had reached and encircled a wire leading to the telegraph pole and wild roses were tight delicious little pink buds that would open later into flat disappointing faded stares. On the bank purple vetches draped on yellow ragwort and a dragonfly, its long striped body quivering, its gauze wings tipped, settled for a moment among the bitter scent of Queen Anne's lace.

The road was long, straight, white and dusty. The early morning sun was behind me, hot on my back. I felt languid, my body relaxed and slightly damp with sweat. In the distance was a slight haze, low down, a warning of more heat to come, and in the haze a black figure suddenly appeared rising from the mist. It was a blurred dark rod, like something veiled, cloaked, right at the end, a long way off. It became a definite shape. It came towards me. I walked on. I passed Mrs. Kerrison's. It was a tall man in dark clothes. We drew nearer. He walked lounging, sauntering. A black hat, the brim low, was down over his eyes. My heart stopped. It stood suspended. The world waited. Then the pumping started, warm, flooding, rising in my body. My feet rushed, my arms opened. I walked slowly, my eyes down, careful not to look, my face breaking into an uncontrollable smile. I watched the hedge as I walked, the sky, the white clouds drifting. I could hear his footsteps, louder than mine. He was there, right before me. I lifted my eyes, they were heavy, from his black shoes, his dark suit, to his face shaded by the large brim. I felt the blood run from my head and my face whiten.

"Why, if it isn't little Ann Fielding."

"Rex."

"Oh, no, it's Mrs. Hales now, isn't it?"

"Rex, you're back."

"No, I'm not. I'm miles away." His eyes were half closed, caressing under the dark hat. I had never seen him in a hat before. In its black shadow he was mysterious, secret.

"Well, how's life treating you?"

"I've missed you, Rex."

He laughed, his white teeth gleaming in his red face. "Not for long. You didn't waste much time marrying your old man."

"It was because you went away."

"Oh, I don't blame you. He was a good catch."

"Why did you go away? Why did you leave me, Rex?"

He laughed easily. "I didn't leave you particularly, I just went. I'm off again soon, in a week or two, going abroad. This little old country's too small for me. Just come to see the old folks, to say ta-ta."

"No, Rex. Oh, no, Rex."

"No, Rex! Yes, Rex!"

"You can't go."

"What's stopping me?"

"You can't leave me again."

He laughed and looked up the road as though he was going.

"Look who's talking! In her nice cushy place with her nice rich husband."

"It doesn't mean anything, Rex. I've thought about you all the time—" He was going to leave me, this time for ever—the pain, the emptiness, stretched, unendurable.

"Couldn't we meet. Just once—just to talk—like we used to?"

"Now then, you're a nice one. I shouldn't h' thought it. What's the old man goin' t' say?"

"He needn't know. Just once, Rex. Tonight, at Foxes Copse."

"Oh, well"—he started to walk away—"I may be along there—"

"What time?"

"Oh, when it's dark. About ten t-half past."

I stood watching him walk away. It did not occur to me to walk back with him. He wore his best navy suit and a red tie. I was meeting him tonight at Foxes Copse. I savoured it. I held it, careful not to break it. I walked slowly home.

When it was nearly dark, I took a torch and went to get my bicycle. I hadn't ridden it since having the car, and the seat was dusty. I found an old rag and gave it a quick flick, then wheeled it onto the gravel. There were footsteps crunching, coming nearer. I put my foot onto the pedal in frantic haste, then a voice said, "This is something new, isn't it?"

Bernard stood in shadow. I could not see him.

"I thought I'd just go for a spin. It's such a lovely night."

"If I had a bicycle, I'd come with you."

He's going to say we'll both go in the car. Oh, don't let him say it! Don't let him say it!

"Well, you haven't, have you?"

My heart beat. I swung myself up.

"I'll be off. I won't be long." I sped down the drive. Behind me, in the darkness, he was watching.

It was cool and fresh after the heat of the day. There was quietness with just the sound of my tires and the half arc of my light in front of me. I stopped with the black mass of Foxes Copse on my right and wheeled my bicycle up a little rise into a small clearing. I put out the light, sat on the ground and waited. In the stillness there were tiny sounds—a faint rustle, and a twig snapped perhaps under the weight of a badger or a hare. Now that my eyes were accustomed, the sky was not black but grey, and through the dark crisscross of branches the wood thinned and I could see the wide meadow and the clear sky beyond. There bats circled silently and dipped and suddenly, quite near me, making my heart jump, birds quarrelled and squawked with a tremendous flutter before quietening again, their differences settled. One huge star shone in the sky. I crossed my fingers and whispered the old rhyme, "Star light, star bright—" I closed my eyes and concentrated intensely.

I watched the tree trunks like black pillars against the grey. Right at the far end of the long narrow copse was an opening arched like the doorway of a cathedral. Its perfection was marred by a black stump at one side. Was it a stump? It had blurred outlines and the height of a tall thin man. Sudden panic rose blinding in my chest. My nails dug into the damp grass. If it should move, I would scream, scream— Had it moved? Wasn't the top a fraction away? Lights were coming, the sound of a car. I ran into the road. He sat there smiling. The same old black car, the same . . .

"I may as well back in here for a while."

I was in, in the close darkness; he was here, warm, breathing. His arms were round me and I closed my eyes, something dying down, relaxing into peace. I had come home. This was rest, this was heaven. If we could just keep like this with his arms round my shoulders, my head hidden in his neck, for ever and ever.

He lifted me roughly, his hand on my leg.

"No, Rex, no."

"Aw, come. Not up to y' old games, are you? You're a married woman now—"

"No, Rex, please, Rex. Can't we just sit here and—"

Bernard. What was Bernard doing? I didn't want it like this, I wanted Rex and I to be married, I wanted to give myself to him, to know him utterly, to know the depths of his mind, to find out what lay behind the secret look.

"Rex, when my husband dies—if he dies—will you marry me?"

"What makes you think he's goin' t' die? He can live for years and years."

"He's a lot older than I am. Things happen, anything could happen, would you, Rex?"

"Well, now, the Mill House, all that money, and you, that would be a bit of all right."

I was gazing over his shoulder at the cathedral opening. The black shape was a man. As I looked, he turned, moved back, and was gone. He had been watching, he had been watching all the time. I tore myself away, fright, terror, making my limbs stiff.

"I must go."

"Aw, come on. What did yer come for, to carry on like this?"

"There was a man, he was watching—"

"What of it? Y' get peepin' Toms everywhere."

"But Bernard—" He will find out. Oh, please don't let Bernard think of me like this.

"An old man must expect t' have a flighty wife."

"No, Rex, it's not like that. I can't stop, Rex. When can I see you again?"

"Oh, I don't know. Not much point in it, is there?"

"Yes, Rex." I was out leaning on the car door. "It will be different next time. I promise. Tomorrow night—"

"Aw, no. I can't make it, then or over the weekend. Our gotta go around an' say goodbye t' all the folks. There's a lot t' see to."

"Don't talk like that, Rex. About going away, you know you can't—"

"I'm goin' and no one's goin' t' stop me. What's the use a' me hangin' round here—a little old farm split up into three or four when the old folks die. About a field apiece, I reckon. What does y' ladyship know about that? No, slavin's not for yours truly."

"We'll talk about it. I must see you, Rex. Monday, it's a long way off, but Monday—"

"I may be along."

I switched on the light on my bicycle.

"Monday then, same time."

I raced along the road up the drive. Was someone there?

Someone watching me from the bushes? The house was in darkness. Bernard had gone to bed. I was glad he had gone to bed. I felt that my face must be marked, my hair tousled. I wanted to be alone. I put the bike away and went into the house. My fingers were stiff. I would get a hot drink. I felt cold, frightened. I burst into the kitchen. He sat in the high-backed Windsor armchair by the stove. He was reading, with the dim light of a shaded lamp shining over his shoulder. He looked up with a quizzical questioning look. I stared, my eyes wide, still holding the door handle. Then I felt tears prick and gush and I ran from the room.

All the stars had come out in the dark blue sky. I stood by my bedroom window, trembling. Footsteps were coming up the stairs, one, two, one, two, slowly, heavily. Then they came along the landing and stopped by my door. It was not locked. I put my hands over my mouth. I could hear faint breathing and listening. And then, in the garden, I saw the man. He crossed a little open space, a dark shadow, and now stood in the bushes by the summerhouse. I pushed my hands hard on my teeth to stop the scream. I was pressed, I was being pressed; the man without—and at the door; I was pressed—then balm settled round me, the feathers soft. I turned into them as to my mother. I lay down and the footsteps went away.

Chapter 20

It was midsummer day. The warm still dusk was the best time for fishing. Bernard had gone to some quiet bank and I was alone to clear the supper things. I had pushed everything to the back of my mind, all the events, the girl, the man, nothing about them was sinister, it was all imagination. Rex was home. I savoured it—my body a warm blush. A pile of specimens, clay-covered, waited for me to clean and catalogue. At last the end of the grey liquid gurgled down from the kitchen sink and I went up the stairs with my basket through the empty echoing house to the Upper Crypt. The half skull leered and the girl in the mirror smiled at me for company. I laid the pieces out on the remaining space of black velvet and picked small white cards from their box—Worked flake, flint flake, Upper Palaeolithic or Neolithic flint core, Samian ware, Castor ware, Neolithic ware, relief band amphora. The small fragments were a bumper find; he would be pleased. At last they all lay documented, carrying on the line of broad black-covered, white-grey-studded shelf, where, at the back, were ninth-century wine jars, red painted pottery exported to eastern England, a pitcher late twelfth century possibly imported from Rouen, Ringsdorf ware, St. Neots ware made from the ninth to the twelfth century, and Stamford ware made from 900 to the thirteenth century from middle Jurassic esturine clay.

I went across for another strip of black velvet from the chest beneath the mirror, to lay ready for the next day's long-buried finds. I looked at the girl as I rose. There were the two of us, she and I, living, in the room. I smiled. We looked at each other for several minutes. The need to break the heaviness became imperative, and suddenly I laughed out loud. The sound cracked the silence and I put my face close to the mirror. My warm breath misted the glass. My white teeth gleamed, my lips were red and full. I lowered my lashes provocatively, then raised them from the shine of my clear blue eyes. Suddenly I raced across the room and lifted from their sleep the gold earrings aged a thousand years. I ruffled my hair and hung them from my lobes. My neck was white, my arms rounded. I unbuttoned my frock, snatched the black velvet, and folded it, a frame for my bare shoulders. Then I reached for the stone prong and piled the front of my golden curls high. I stood sideways, looked in the mirror, and gathered my skirts. The room stretched behind me. At the far end the cracked burial urns glimmered. Tarantella! I snapped my fingers, threw back my head and clicked my heels. I twirled and laughed at the girl and she laughed back. Then I opened the door and to ghostly snapping music raced down the stairs. A low white mist covered the garden. I danced with wild gaiety—

The roses loom in pinky shapes,
The starry jasmine is dreaming sweet.
The lawns are spread with softest silk,
Waiting for my lover's feet.

I was waiting for Rex. While I danced, I was waiting for Rex. Through the trees he would come. He would bow and take my hand and we would dance. "You are beautiful," he would say while we danced. "You are beautiful—

Your eyes are like the summer skies,
Your hair, the sun—"

Suddenly it was cold. The gaiety faded. It drained away and left me empty, bare. I buttoned my frock and put the black velvet like a scarf around my neck. I took the comb and earrings and carried them in my hand. My feet were chill, damp with the mist as I wandered along the gravel. Loneliness wrenched, a savage pain. Bernard was fishing on the landing stage. He sat under the dark canopy on the edge, a hunched squat figure on a small folding stool. I stood quietly watching. And I remembered where I had seen the face of the woman. She was the girl on the photograph that had been shown to me by Mrs. Baltrop long ago. Perhaps she was connected with the police although pretending to be something else, and she was hunting Bernard. He had murdered Mr. Montague and somehow the police had got onto the trail. Whether they could hang another person after such a mistake, I did not know, but they would shut him up for ever—the warmth in the crinkled eyes would fade, the dear body grow thin, the sharp mind falter. Although my body yearned for Rex with a hot pain, had always waited for Rex so that I must believe it, I could not let this happen to Bernard. But if he should drown, it would be over in a few minutes—they could do nothing. In the mist-shrouded dusk the only sound was a faint plop and a tiny gurgle of water under the boards. Beyond the dark tunnel was a silver round. It stretched out over the marshes like the opening to a new world. He sat alone above the deep water. If he should fall —if he should die—Rex would marry me. Bernard would not mind dying. "Dying," he had often said, "what is it? Either falling asleep or passing to another world. We are not that important. Why does it worry us?" and "I hope I do not live to be too old. Better just to go while one still has interests, not fade and rot like an old leaf." Even as he falls, and his eyes look up into mine from the water, he will understand and forgive.

It was deadly quiet. There was no plop, and even the gurgle seemed to hush and to be waiting; my heartbeat choking, just a moment's courage and it will be done. I stepped forward. His grey hair came down from under his tweed cap into the folds of his neck. A dark dried stain spread on one shoulder of the gabardine mackintosh. Just one push and it will be over. My arms rose. Behind me was a small sound. It was not a cough, it was a small human noise made deliberately. I turned. A tall grey-haired figure stood in the mist. His arms were outstretched to pull me back and in his eyes was alarm. It was not old Tom; it was Mr. Montague.

Chapter 21

I ran. Terror ran alongside. It ran behind. It carried me. My feet seemed not to touch the ground. I was in the car. It burst into life. I drove through the night. It was as though I had no body, I had no car, just my brain, lit with a searching light penetrating its own mist and everything was clear, everything was clear, clear with a sharpness that cut like a knife, a razor, an edge of fine glass—that turned back the covering like the peel from a fruit and there lay the truth. On the night after I had seen the man and Miranda and later the room had been full of her weeping—while I had been carefully settled to look at the heavy book with its butterflies and flowers—it was old Tom who had been struck and pushed—it was old Tom who had been guided into the deep muddy water under the landing stage with the planks which were then secured. It was old Tom's life that had gushed away under the water and Mr. Montague had taken his place. The chicken and the fruit that I had left on the doorstep that next day had been for his own use, the note for Mrs. Kerrison's eyes to lead her, and the flung fishing gear on the bushes for my notice. The head that I had seen at the window was Mr. Montague's after he was comfortably entrenched at the cottage. Miranda . . .

I saw the fastidious hands.

"One must cast out anything that is soiled—blemished."

I must go to Rex. I must tell Rex. His warmth must help me, hold me. It was dark. My lights lit tree-hung caverns. I drove numbly, my right hand gripped to the wheel, my left half clenched with a strange cutting pain. I swung through the gateway flanked by sagging palings, white flaking from grey. My lights swept over the low thatched farmhouse. The windows were dark, closed, and a collie dog came round the corner, barking. I got out of the car and the dog came growling. I walked straight towards it. Let it tear my flesh. Let its teeth sink into my ankles. The lights lit its strange white walleye, its bared teeth. I walked on. It backed, barking furiously, then turned and ran round the side of the house, its plumed tail waving. I stood on the broken step and knocked on the door. A faint light came on and shone pinkly through the dusty fanlight. There was the crunch of a key and the rattle of a chain. The door opened with a creak of unuse and his mother stood there.

"Is Rex in?"

She stood looking at me, the grey hair, centre-parted, folded down round the fat sallow face, the dirty white apron a sheet around her middle.

"Is Rex in, please?"

She still stared, unsmiling, at this married woman from the big house running after her son. She turned her head.

"Is Rick about?"

A voice answered from the back. "He's out. It's Saturday night."

"Where'd he be? D'yer know?"

"There's a dance on. 'Spect he's at the Hut."

"There's a dance. He's at the Hut."

She shut the door.

The Hut—the familiar tin building alongside the pub. The lights from its windows threw bright lozenges on the flung bicycles and packed old cars. Music came faintly as I crunched across the gravelled yard. I backed and stopped by the side wall of the pub, in its deep shadow, and the music burst louder as I turned off the engine. High above me was a small half-open window, from which pale light streamed over and beyond so that I sat in darkness as beneath a waterfall. I turned down the car window and listened. I was unaware of my body, but my brain was tightened in my head. The noises were loud, sharp, the smell of beer from the pub a wave of nausea. There was the tiny ping of darts on the board, the clang of the till.

"Give us a song, Harry."

"Yer, come on, Harry boy."

"What d'yer want?"

" 'John Brown's Body.' Come on, Harry. 'John Brown's Body.' "

"All right, everyone, are yer ready, Frank? Come on, Mrs. D, pipe up, John Brown's body—"

A piano was thumped to a tinkle of sound.

"John Brown's body lies a-mouldin' in the grave—John Brown's body—"

A man lurched from the door grinning. He steadied himself against the wing of the car, then went behind. There was the stream and stench of urine, then he passed back buttoning his trousers.

The mist had gone. The night was clear black.

There was a lull in the music from the Hut, then a clear voice said, "Take your partners for the Paul Jones."

Stamping, shouting, shrill whistles bounded from the tin, then the music started again.

Suddenly, quite near, another voice in the pub said, "Time, gentlemen, please."

"Half a mo, pal, give us a chance—"

"Give us time t' drink up."

"Gotta be particular. Young Simpson, the new bob, was round here last week."

"Yer, he's a sharp 'un. Not like old Pearson, dead an' gone. Dear old pal, jolly old pal—"

"Come on, cut the singin'. There's another day tomorrow."

"Well—good night, Harry."

"Good night, George."

A door slammed shut and was bolted. Two men came behind and urinated. One or two cars moved away and the light above me snapped off.

The dance would go on, an hour, another two hours?

A couple came out and stood pressed against the wall. Then another couple came through the lighted open door giggling.

"Cor, look at them!" They passed round the side into the darkness.

Suddenly, my heart leapt. Just in front of where the couple were leaning stood Rex's car, a big black shape. Perhaps the light from the window had prevented me seeing it, or it had been hidden by one of the men's cars from the pub.

Breath, choking, rose into my throat. I shut my eyes tight. He is here. He is in the Hut. Realize it. Concentrate on it. A few yards from you, he is here, his strong body, his caressing eyes, his warm arms. They will be round you and nothing will matter, nothing else will matter. If only the couple would go. Let him come out alone—don't let him come out with a crowd. I cannot run to him, I cannot call in front of . . .

The couple straightened and smoothed themselves down. She combed her hair and he held a tiny mirror while she powdered her nose, then, slowly, they strolled back into the Hut.

There was no one. The music was blaring. Just for one second the yard, the gravel was empty. There might not be another—I ran, I sped to the black shape. I opened the door—I was in. I sank onto the broad back seat, trembling, my heart hammering. I put up my feet and lay down, pulling the black rug over me, the old familiar rug that smelt of dogs, oil, and linseed. Now I would wait. Already I felt calmer, the old Ford, like a hand, holding me. I ran my finger along the leather of the front seat. Here his back rests—his hands touch that wheel.

I lay back and closed my eyes. It is all a bad dream. If I sleep, I will wake and it will have been a dream. I am thirteen and I shall wake at the Mill House to the noise of the weir and the sunlight. Miranda will be bending over me.

"Wake up, sleepyhead."

"I have had such a dream, such a bad dream, Miranda."

There were light footsteps on the gravel. Rex was coming towards the car. With him was a girl. She was thin and fair-haired. His arm was round her, his hand on her thigh. He was looking down at her with his caressing look, smiling his secret smile.

I pulled the rug over my head. Oh, God. Please, God. The girl opened the door at the front and got in.

"We might as well get in the back."

"You and your back seat." The girl laughed. "Here I am and here I sit."

"Oh, well—"

He went round to the other side, got in and slammed the door. There was movement and giggles.

"No, Rex."

"Come on, Bess. We're soon goin' to be hitched. What do you think I gave you the ring for?"

"Plenty of time for that when we are."

"Don't be hard on a chap, Bess."

"I'm not your woman up at the Mill House."

"What's she got to do with it?"

"I'm not having you running after her, and then trying t' make a fuss of me."

"I don't care if I never see her again. I'm sick t' death of her. Come on, Bess. I tell you I'm sick t' death of her —always mealing around. I bet she'd do anything I asked her. I bet she'd even bump the old man off if I asked her."

"With all that money you would be all right."

"With her thrown in? Now the money and you, that would be a different maria."

"Some hope of that. Listen!" There was silence. "That's the last dance."

"Aw, come on, let's go. I don't feel like dancing."

"There's our coats."

"Well, you go in and get 'um an' I'll stop here."

"What! Catch me going in the gents. You can go if you like."

"I'm not goin' in the ladies. Aw, come on, let's get it over with."

The doors slammed. The yard was empty. I walked across the gravel slowly, deliberately, careful not to fall. The car swept me away, away from the lights into the darkness. I stopped by the side of the road under black dripping trees. The numbness was going, the blood running again in my veins bringing creeping burning agony. I folded my arms and bent, rocking, nursing the pain, holding it, protecting it, and suddenly my body burst with sweat. It ran, stinging, into my dry eyes, and then I was icy-cold. I opened the fourth and fifth fingers of my left hand and there, where the nails had dug, embedded in the bleeding palm, were fragments of the earrings. A pity, I thought vaguely; broken after a thousand years. I started the engine and drove into the night. I had no one to turn to, nowhere to go. No one; in a blinding flash I saw myself —the secret look—I laughed, it hurt my chest, my sides. The tears rolled down my face. I had fastened the dream of youth, the idea of love, on this creature. There was no mystery, there was nothing. I would drive on and on. I would drive into the cold, cold sea, the car would fly through the air, and then it would fall and the waters would close over me. I would walk, a tart, in the bright lights, with paint on my face, a look in my eyes. It would be lonelier than the sea—lonelier—my mother—my mother had said, "When he was gone, it was lonely, there is nothing worse than loneliness." I drew up at a gate. I turned the car round. I drove back along the roads. I would go back home. I would tell my husband everything. I would lay the burden down, face whatever there was to face. The Mill House—my lights lit the trees by the drive, the hanging branches, and before me, perhaps a trick of colour on glistening leaves, a ghost danced on sandalled feet. She turned, her wide skirts swirling, her gipsy curls all tumbling and her black eyes flashed a question. Then the radiance faded. A damp warm cheek was pressed to mine—or was it my own tears? I tried to speak but no sound came. How does one speak to a ghost, how does one say forgive me, forgive me, Miranda . . .?

Chapter 22

I burst into the kitchen. Bernard would keep me safe. Bernard would—he was sitting by the stove. Facing him sat the woman. I turned and ran up to my room and threw myself onto the bed in the darkness. I lay pressed to the counterpane, face down, my hands gripping the folds. Then the door opened softly, the shaded bedside light clicked on, and there was silence. I turned, looking up. The woman stood there. In her hand was a tray with a pot of coffee, a large glass of brandy and a plate of sandwiches. I turned again and hid my face. There was the sound of the small table and chair being brought forward.

"Come," she said, "drink this." I pressed my face further into the warm safe bed.

"I expect you wonder who I am."

She spoke slowly, softly. I knew that she was making conversation to give me time.

"I am a private detective. I was hired by your husband."

They were not hunting Bernard. Of course they were not hunting Bernard.

"My father was a chief constable and I always wanted to join the force, but they do not take women. I think they should. Later I was lamed in a car accident."

I heard the clink of sugar tongs, the pouring, and smelt the strong black coffee.

"Then my brother and I set up this detective agency."

A little pocket of peace came into the dreadful tangle in my mind.

"Your husband approached me because he suspected. He caught sight of Mr. Montague one night in the grounds. I have found out that he always fished at night. But your husband had to have proof. If the police, or I, had gone, broken into the cottage, which of course we could not do without evidence, the act of being old Tom would have been put on. So I have been hiding, and waiting, to take photographs. I was behind him when he frightened you."

I turned and looked at her, raising myself on my elbow.

"You saw?"

"Yes." She put her arm round me and lifted me up. "Drink this and you will feel better."

"You saw what I was about to do?"

"Some things are best forgotten."

I swung my legs to the floor and sat sipping the burning liquid.

"I could see," she went on, "that you were terrified, and I would have run after you, but he collapsed, a heart attack, and died soon after. He said three words, "Poor little Ann.' "

"He betrayed himself to save me."

I drank and ate the sandwiches automatically, too numb for tears.

"No. I knew before. I had some good photographs."

"Nevertheless he did. He would not know that. He instinctively betrayed himself to save me."

"Now"—she got up briskly—"come down and see your husband. I must go. By the way"—she smiled—"my name is Ann too."

Bernard was sitting in the kitchen. He rose, smiling, his eyes crinkling in their stars, and led me to the warmth.

"I thanked God when I saw you. We were wondering what to do."

"Ann has gone," I said. I sat on the rug and put my arms on his knees. His hand fondled my hair.

"Tell me about it," I said.

"I would have told you before. But I didn't want to worry you, bring back old memories."

"You should have told me. You have kept me a child. I am not a child."

"No. But you have gone through dreadful things. It's extraordinary—poor old crafty Montague. I never thought for one moment. It never occurred to me that he was the same Montague. I knew him at Cambridge. He was quite a bit older, a don, while I was an undergraduate. I was engaged to Stephanie. I felt flattered and honoured by his attention and company until I realized what he was after. He took her away from me. I wondered for a time what sort of life she led with him." He was quiet for a moment, but his hand still brushed my hair. "The cold cunning discerning devil. But then I put it all behind me. I sealed the mementoes in the bureau in my parents' home and went abroad. About a month ago there was an article in the daily paper with a photograph of Mr. Montague. I was absolutely astonished. And by some strange coincidence, that night I caught sight of him in the grounds from my window. Then of course I was certain, but I had to get proof."

The brandy had gone pleasantly to my head. The unravelling, the solving had untwisted a tight knot. I pulled Bernard's hand to his knee and laid my cheek upon it. I closed my eyes. All I wanted was that his arms should hold me tightly and warmly until morning.

"Of course we must now go to the police," he said.

"No!" I sat up violently. "No, I could not bear all that again."

"I am afraid you must"—he spoke gently—"to clear Miranda's name."

"No. What good will it do?"

She is dead—Miranda—

"I think, in a few days, you will feel differently."

"No, I shall not."

"We shall see. Now"—he got up and lifted me—"come to bed."

I have finished, and the wave of deep water, the translucent greenness, fresh dampness, and my lost innocence fade and leave me with this arid brightness. I wheel myself, my hands gripping the sides, with my arms, which have become stronger since the accident, to the bureau. The cuttings are there, yellowing at the bottom of a pile of papers.

DEATHS

the areas	Clarke - On June 23, at the	One hun
nes valid	Cottage Hospital, Bincome,	timers
nce of a	George, aged 82 years.	grand t
or the re	Hambling - On June 21st sud-	The get
eals; the	denly, at his home Mill Cot-	social
damage to	tage, Little Snelling, Thomas,	wich br
ucational	aged 72 years. For 48 years	directi
Dill had	gardener at the Mill House,	chester
the House	Little Snelling.	of them
when it	Hancer- On June 21st at	with th
Lord Cran	Brook Farm, Walton, Han-	them st
by the	nah, dearly loved mother of	old Gre
interests	Sarah and Charles, and	include
eels that	beloved wife of Donald. Flow-	Mr Robe
existing	ers to be sent to W. E. Smith &	as an e

EAST ANGLIAN DAILY NEWS

June 26, 1933

	Sensational Development	
attests to	Funeral Stopped at Little Snelling	Last n
of the	Following information re-	contro
near the	ceived, the funeral purported	a form
yester-	to be that of Thomas Ham-	anarch
it had put	bling of Mill Cottage, Little	protes
the basic	Snelling, was stopped by po-	thousa
them a	lice yesterday.	six st
between it	Sensational developments	freef
not apply	are expected. Little Snelling	ransom
to work	came into the news when, in	Banker
workers in	1927, Miranda Montague was	still
concerned	tried before the Rt. Hon. Lord	with a
half of	Justice Harold and convicted	joined

I clip them after the last page in the lined exercise book and put the twelve thin books in the bureau. I will tie them and glue the drawer up tomorrow.